*Leon* **wanted** *her to be his baby's mother.*

That had to mean something, didn't it?

He was the most marvelous man. To think he trusted her with his prized possession!

Even if she was a virgin who'd had no experience with men, she could do the mothering part right. Maybe their marriage would help heal the wound between Leon and his family.

Marriage to Leon would ensure a close relationship with Belle's mother for the rest of their lives.

But what if Leon met another woman and fell in love?

She knew the answer to that. It would kill her. But would their marriage be so different from the many marriages where one of the partners strayed? It was a fact of life that millions of married men and women had affairs. There were no guarantees.

By the time morning came, she'd gone back and forth so many times she was physically and emotionally exhausted. But one thing stood out above all else. The thought of going back to her life in New York sounded like living death....

Dear Reader,

About a year ago I was watching a documentary about adoption. It followed the lives of two different women who'd been adopted and wanted to meet their birth mother. In both cases the reunions brought joy to begin with. The birth mothers now knew what had happened to the baby they'd had to give up. The birth children now had answers about their origins and the family they came from. This documentary picked up on their lives five years later. In the first case, both parties had kept up a relationship. In the second case, neither party continued to stay in contact. The documentary discussed the reasons why and why not.

I found it so fascinating that the idea for a story began to grow in my mind and became *A Marriage Made in Italy*. In this love story I have incorporated some of the things I learned in the documentary about the expectations of the adopted child in relation to the adoptive parent, as well as to the birth parent, with all their attendant intricacies.

Enjoy!

Rebecca Winters

# REBECCA WINTERS

*A Marriage Made in Italy*

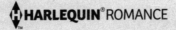

Recycling programs
for this product may
not exist in your area.

ISBN-13: 978-0-373-74253-0

A MARRIAGE MADE IN ITALY

First North American Publication 2013

Copyright © 2013 by Rebecca Winters

**HARLEQUIN**®

www.Harlequin.com

**Printed in U.S.A.**

**Rebecca Winters,** whose family of four children has now swelled to include five beautiful grandchildren, lives in Salt Lake City, Utah, in the land of the Rocky Mountains. With canyons and high alpine meadows full of wildflowers, she never runs out of places to explore. They, plus her favourite vacation spots in Europe, often end up as backgrounds for her romance novels, because writing is her passion, along with her family and church.

Rebecca loves to hear from readers. If you wish to email her, please visit her website, www.cleanromances.com.

## Recent books by Rebecca Winters

ALONG CAME TWINS... *
BABY OUT OF THE BLUE *
THE COUNT'S CHRISTMAS BABY
THE RANCHER'S HOUSEKEEPER
A BRIDE FOR THE ISLAND PRINCE
SNOWBOUND WITH HER HERO
HER ITALIAN SOLDIER
HER DESERT PRINCE

*Tiny Miracles*

Other titles by Rebecca Winters available in ebook format.

# CHAPTER ONE

BELLE PETERSON LEFT the cell phone store she managed, and took a bus to the law office of Mr. Earl Harmon in downtown Newburgh, New York. The secretary showed her into the conference room. She discovered her thirty-year-old, divorced sibling, Cliff, had already arrived and was sitting at the oval table with a mulish look on his face, daring her to speak to him. She hadn't seen him since their parents' funeral six months ago.

On the outside he was blond and quite good-looking, but his facade hid a troubled soul. He'd been angry enough after his wife had left him, but the deaths of their parents in a fatal car crash meant he was now on his own. Today Belle felt Cliff's antipathy more strongly than usual and chose a seat around the other side of the table without saying a word.

Now twenty-four and single, she had been

adopted fourteen years ago. The children at the Newburgh Church Orphanage had liked her, as had the sisters. But out in the real world, Belle felt she was unlovable, and worked hard at her job to gain the respect of her peers. Her greatest pain was never to know the mother who'd given birth to her. To have no identity was an agony she'd had to live with every day of her life.

The sisters who ran the orphanage had told Belle that Mrs. Peterson had been able to have only one child. She'd finally prevailed on her husband to adopt the brunette girl, Belle, who had no last name. This was Belle's chance to have a mother, but no bonding ever took place. From the day she'd been taken home, Cliff had been cruel to her, making her life close to unbearable at times.

"Good morning."

Belle was so deep in thought over the past, she didn't realize Mr. Harmon had come into the room. She shook his hand.

"I'm glad you two could arrange to meet here at the same time. I have some bad news and some good. Let's start with the bad first."

The familiar scowl on Cliff's face spoke volumes.

"As you know, there was no insurance,

therefore the home you grew up in was sold to pay off the multitude of debts. The good news is you've each been given fifteen hundred dollars from the auction of the furnishings. I have checks for you." He passed them out.

Cliff shot to his feet. *"That's it?"* Belle heard panic beneath his anger. She knew he'd been waiting to come into some money, if only to make up delinquent alimony payments. She hadn't expected anything herself and rejoiced to receive this check, which she clutched in her hand before putting it in her purse.

"I'm sorry, Mr. Peterson, but everything went to pay off your father's debts and cover the burial costs. Please accept my sincere sympathy at the passing of your parents. I wish both of you the very best."

"Thank you, Mr. Harmon," Belle said, when Cliff continued to remain silent.

"If you ever need my help, feel free to call." The attorney smiled at her and left the room. The second he was gone, an explosion of venom escaped Cliff's lips. He shot her a furious glance.

"It's all *your* fault. If Mom hadn't nagged Dad for a daughter, there would have been more money and we wouldn't be in this mess. Why don't you go back to Italy where you belong?"

Her heart suddenly pounded with dizzying intensity. "What did you say?"

"You heard me. Dad never wanted you."

"You think I didn't know that?" She moved closer to her brother, holding her breath. "Are you saying I came from Italian parents?" All along she'd thought the sisters at the orphanage might have named her for the fairy-tale character, or else she came from French roots.

Her whole life she'd been praying to find out her true lineage, and she'd gone to the orphanage many times seeking information. But every time she did, she'd been told they couldn't help her. Nadine, her adoptive mother, had never revealed the truth to her, but Belle had heard Cliff's slip and refused to let it go.

He averted his eyes and wheeled around to leave, but she raced ahead of him and blocked the door. At twenty-four, Belle was no longer frightened of him. Before they left this office and parted ways forever, she had to ask the question that had been inscribed on her mind and heart from the time she knew she was an orphan. "What else do you know about my background?"

Cliff flashed her a mocking smile. "Now that Dad's no longer alive, how much money are you willing to pay me for the information?"

She could hardly swallow before she opened her purse and pulled out the check. In a trembling voice she said, "I'd give you *this* to learn anything that could help me know my roots." While he watched, she drew out a pen and endorsed it over to him.

For the first time since she'd known him, his eyes held a puzzled look rather than an angry one. "You'd give up that much money just to know about someone who didn't even want you?"

"Yes," she whispered, fighting tears. "It's not important if they didn't want me. I just need to know who I am and where I came from. If you know anything, I beg you to tell me." Taking a leap of faith, she handed him the check.

He took it from her and studied it for a moment. "You always were pathetic," he muttered.

"So you don't know anything and were just teasing me with your cruelty? That doesn't really surprise me. Go on. Keep it. I never thought we'd get that much money from the auction, anyway. You're one of the lucky people who grew up knowing your parents. Too bad they're gone and you're all alone now. Knowing how it feels, I wouldn't wish that on anyone, not even you."

Belle opened the door, and had started to leave when she heard him say, "The old man said your last name was the same as the redheaded smart-mouth he hated in high school."

Her heart thundered. She spun around. "Who was that?"

"Frankie Donatello."

*"Donatello?"*

"Yeah. One day I heard Mom and Dad arguing about you. That's when it came out. He said he wished they'd never adopted that Italian girl's brat. After he left for work, I told Mom she ought to send you back to where you came from, because you weren't wanted. She said that would be impossible because it was someplace in Italy."

*What?* "Where in Italy?" Belle demanded.

"I don't know. It sounded something like Remenee."

"How did he find out? The sisters told me it was a closed adoption."

"How the hell do *I* know?"

It didn't matter, because joy lit up Belle's insides. Her leap of faith had paid off! Without conscious thought she reached out and hugged him so hard she almost knocked him over. "Thank you! I know you hate me, but I love you for this and forgive every mean thing you ever said or did to me. Goodbye, Cliff."

She rushed out of the law office to the bus stop and rode back to work. After nodding to the sales reps, she disappeared into the back room and looked for a map of Italy on the computer. She was trembling so violently she could hardly work the keyboard.

As she scrolled down the list of cities and towns that popped up, the name Rimini appeared, most closely matching "Remenee." The blood pounded in her ears when she looked it up and discovered it was a town of a hundred forty thousand along the Adriatic. It was in the province of Rimini.

Quickly, she scanned the month's schedule of vacations for the employees. They all had one week off in summer and one in winter. Belle was on summer break from college, where she went to night school. Her vacation would be coming up the third week of June, ten days away.

Without hesitation she booked a flight from New York City to Rimini, Italy, and made arrangements for a rental car. She

chose the cheapest flight, with two stop-
overs, and made a reservation at a pension
that charged only twenty-eight dollars a day.
No phone, no TV. The coed bathroom was
down the hall. Sounded like the orphanage.
That was fine with her. A bed was all she
needed.

Since she'd been saving her money, and
roomed with two other girls, she'd managed
to put away a modest nest egg. All these
years she'd been guarding it for something
important, never dreaming the money would
ever help her to find her mother.

"Belle?"

She lifted her head and smiled politely at
her colleague. "Yes, Mac?"

"How about going for pizza after we lock
up tonight?"

"I'm sorry, but I have other plans."

"You always say that. How can someone
so gorgeous turn me down? Come on. How
about it?"

Her new assistant manager, transferred in
from another store, was good-looking and a
real barracuda in sales, but he irritated her
by continually trying to get her to go out
with him.

"Mac? I've told you already that I'm not
interested."

"Some of the guys call you the Ice Queen." He never gave up.

"Really. Anything else you want to say to me before you finish the inventory?"

She heard a smothered imprecation before the door closed. Good. Maybe she *was* an ice queen. Fine! So far she hadn't seen examples of love in her personal life and didn't expect to.

Her birth parents had given her away. Her adoptive parents had suffered through an unhappy marriage. Her adoptive brother was already divorced, and angry. He'd used her pretty mercilessly as an emotional punching bag. Belle always felt she was on the outside looking in, but never being part of a whole.

She thought about the single girls at the store, who all struggled to find good dates and were usually miserable with the ones they landed. Two of the four guys were married. One of them was having an affair. The other was considering divorce. The other two were players. Both spent their money on clothes and cars.

Her own roommates were still single and terrified they would end up alone. It was all they talked about when the three of them went running in the mornings.

Belle didn't worry about being alone. That

had been her state from the moment she was born. The few dates she'd accepted here and there outside the workplace had fizzled. It was probably her fault, because she didn't feel very lovable and wasn't as confident as she needed to be. Marriage wasn't an option for her.

She didn't trust any relationship to last, and cut it off early. Belle hadn't met a man she'd cared enough about to imagine going to bed with. No doubt her mother had experimented, and gotten caught with no resources but the church orphanage to help her. Belle refused to get into that circumstance.

What she *could* depend on was her career, which gave her the stability she craved after being dependent on the orphanage and her adoptive parents. She was a free agent now. Her store had been number one in the region for two years. Soon she hoped to be promoted to upper-level management in the company.

But first she would take her precious vacation time to try to find her mother. If Cliff had gotten it wrong or misunderstood, then maybe the trip would be for nothing, but Belle had to think positive thoughts. Romantic Italy, the world of Michelangelo, gondolas and the famous tenor Pavarotti, had always sounded as delightful and as faraway as the moon. Incredible to believe she'd actually be flying there in ten days.

Tomorrow she'd see about equipping herself with a company GSM phone and SIM card, the kind with a quad-band. Once in Rimini, she'd find a local library and work from the latest city phone directory to do her research.

She was in the midst of making a mental list of things she'd need when Rod, one of the reps, suddenly burst in on her. "Hey, boss? Can you come out in front? An angry client just threw his cell phone at Sheila and is demanding satisfaction. He said it broke after he bought it."

She smiled. "If it wasn't broken, it is now. No problem." No problem at all on the first red-letter day of her life. "I'll be right there."

It was seven in the morning when thirty-three-year-old Leonardo Rovere di Malatesta, the elder son of Count Sullisto Malatesta of Rimini, finally got his little six-month-old Concetta to sleep. The doctor said she'd caught a bug, and he'd prescribed medicine to bring down her temperature. It was now two degrees lower than it had been at midnight, and she hadn't thrown up again, *grazie a Dio!*

After he'd walked the floor with her all night in an attempt to comfort her, he was exhausted. The dog ought to be exhausted, too. Rufo was a brown roan Spinone, a wedding gift from his wife's father.

Rufo had been devoted to Benedetta and had transferred his allegiance to Concetta when Leon had returned from the hospital without his wife. Since that moment, their dog had never let the baby out of his sight. Leon was deeply moved by such a show of love, and patted the animal's head.

There was no way he'd be going in to the bank today. Talia and Rufo would watch over his daughter while he slept. The forty-year-old nanny had been with him since Benedetta had died in childbirth, and was devoted to his precious child. If the baby's fever spiked again, he could count on her to waken him immediately.

He kissed Concetta's head with its fine, dark blond hair, and laid her in the crib on her back, out of habit. She never stayed in that position for long. Her lids hid brown eyes dark as poppy throats. She had Benedetta's coloring and facial features. Leon loved this child in a way he hadn't thought possible. Her presence and demanding needs filled the aching loneliness in his heart for the wife he'd lost.

After tiptoeing out of the nursery, he told Talia he was going to bed, then went to find his housekeeper, who'd always worked for his mother's family. She and Talia were cousins, and he trusted them implicitly.

"Simona? I've turned off my cell phone. If someone needs me, knock on my door."

The older woman nodded before Leon headed for his bedroom. He was so exhausted he didn't remember his head touching the pillow. The relief of knowing the baby's fever had broken helped him to fall into a deep sleep.

When he heard a tap on his door later, he checked his watch. He'd slept seven hours and couldn't believe it was already midafternoon! He came awake immediately, fearing something was wrong.

"Simona? Is Concetta worse?" he called out.

"No, no. She has recovered. Talia is feeding her." Relief swamped him a second time. "Your assistant at the bank asked if you would phone him at your convenience."

*"Grazie."* Leon levered himself off the bed and headed for the shower, surprised

that Berto would call the villa. Normally he would leave a message on Leon's cell. Maybe he had.

After he'd shaved and dressed, Leon reached for his phone. There was a message from his father asking him to join the family for dinner.

Not tonight.

Another message came from his friend Vito, in Rome. Leon would phone him before he went to bed.

Nothing from Berto.

Leon walked into the kitchen, where he found Talia feeding plums from a jar to his daughter, who was propped in her high chair. Rufo sat on the floor with his tail moving back and forth, watching with those human-like eyes.

Concetta's sweet little face broke into a smile the second she saw her father, and she waved her hands. Whenever she did that, it made him thankful he was alive. He felt her forehead, pleased to note her fever was gone.

"I do believe you're much better, *il mio tesoro*. As soon as I make a few phone calls, you and I are going to go out on the patio and play." It overlooked his private stretch of beach with its fine golden sand. Concetta was strong and loved to stand in it in her bare feet if he braced her.

Yesterday he'd bought a new set of stacking buckets for her, but she hadn't felt well enough to be interested. Now that her health was improved, he couldn't wait to see what she'd do with them. First, however, he phoned his father to explain that the baby had been sick and needed to be put down early.

When Leon heard the disappointment in his voice, he made arrangements for dinner the following evening *if* she was all better. With that accomplished he called his secretary at the bank.

"Berto? I sent you a text message telling you my daughter was ill. Is there a problem that can't wait until tomorrow?"

"No, no. I'll talk to you in the morning, provided the *bambina* is better."

Leon rubbed the pad of his thumb along his lower lip. "You wouldn't have phoned if you didn't think it was important."

"At first I thought it was."

"But now you've changed your mind?" Berto was being uncharacteristically cryptic.

"*Sì*. It can wait until tomorrow. *Ciao,* Leon."

His assistant actually hung up on him!

Leon clicked off and eyed the baby, who'd eaten all her plums and seemed perfectly content playing with her fingers.

"Talia, something has come up at the bank. I'll run into town and be back within the hour. Tell Simona to phone me if there's the slightest problem."

"The little one will be fine."

He kissed his daughter's cheek. "I'll see you soon."

After changing into a suit, Leon alerted his bodyguard before leaving the villa. He drove his black sports car into the most celebrated seaside resort city in Europe, curious to understand what was going on with Berto.

After pulling around to the back of the ornate, two-story Renaissance building, partially bombed during World War II and later reconstructed, he let himself in the private entrance reserved for him and his family. He took the marble staircase two steps at a time to his office on the next floor, where he served as assets manager for Malatesta Banking, one of the two top banking institutions in Italy.

Under his father's brilliant handling as wealth manager, they'd grown to twenty-five thousand employees. With his brother, Dante, overseeing the broker-dealer department, business was going well despite Italy's economic downturn. If the call from Berto meant any kind of trouble, Leon intended to get to the bottom of it pronto.

His redheaded assistant was on a call when Leon walked into his private suite of rooms. Judging from his expression, Berto was surprised to see him. He rang off quickly and got to his feet. "I didn't know you were coming."

Leon's hands went to his hips. "I didn't expect you to hang up so quickly from our earlier conversation. I want to know what's wrong. Don't tell me again it's nothing. Which of the accounts is in trouble?"

Berto looked flustered. "It has nothing to do with the accounts. A woman came to the bank earlier today after being sent from Donatello Diamonds on the Corso D'Augosto."

"And?" Leon demanded, sensing his assistant's hesitation.

"Marcello in Security called up here, asking for you to handle the inquiry, since your father wasn't available. The manager at Donatello's told her she would have to speak to someone at the bank. That's when I called you.

"But after I heard it was some American wanting information about the Donatello family, I figured it was a foreign reporter snooping around. At that point I decided not to bother you any more about it."

Leon frowned in puzzlement. Someone wanting to do legitimate business would have made an appointment with him or his father and left their full name.

*Was* it one of the paparazzi posing as an American tourist in order to dig up news about the family? Leon's relatives had to be on constant alert against the media wanting to rake up old scandal to sell papers.

Leon had seen it all and viewed life with a cynical eye. It was what came from being a Malatesta, hated in earlier centuries and still often an object of envy.

"When I couldn't get you or your father, I tried your brother, but he's out of town. I told Marcello this person would have to leave a name and phone number. With your daughter sick, I didn't consider this an emergency, but I still wanted you to be informed."

"I appreciate that. You handled it perfectly. Do you have the information she left?"

Berto handed the notepaper to him. "That's the phone number and address of the Pensione Rosa off the Via Vincenza Monti. The woman's name is Belle. Marcello said she's in her early twenties, and with her long dark hair and blue eyes, more than lives up to her name. When she approached him, he thought she was a film star."

Naturally. Didn't the devil usually appear in the guise of a beautiful woman? Of course she didn't leave a last name....

"Good work, Berto. Tell no one else about this. See you tomorrow."

More curious than ever, Leon left the bank. A few minutes later he discovered the small lodging down an alley, half hidden by the other buildings. He parked and entered. No one was around, so he pressed the buzzer at the front desk. In a moment a woman older than Simona came out of an alcove.

"I'm Rosa. If you need a room, we're full, s*ignore*."

Leon handed her the paper. "You have a woman named Belle registered here?"

"*Sì.*" With that staccato answer he realized he wouldn't be learning her guest's last name the easy way.

"Could you ring her room, *per favore?*"

"No phone in the rooms."

He might have known, considering the low price for accommodations listed on the back wall. "Do you know if she's in?"

"She went out several hours ago and hasn't returned."

He spied a chair against the wall, next to an end table with a lamp on it. "I'll wait."

The woman scrutinized him. "Leave me your name and number and she can call you from the desk here after she returns."

"I'll take my chances and see if she comes in."

With a shrug of her ample shoulders, the woman disappeared through the alcove.

Rather than sit here for what might be hours, he phoned one of his security people to do surveillance. When Ruggio arrived, Leon gave him the American woman's description and said he wanted to be notified as soon as she showed up.

With that taken care of, he walked out to the alley and got in his car. He was halfway to the villa when his cell phone rang. It was Ruggio. Leon clicked on. "What's happening?"

"The woman fitting the description you gave me just entered. She's driving a rental car from the airport."

"Which agency?"

When Ruggio gave him the particulars, Leon told him to stay put until he got there. On the way back to the pension, he called the rental agency and asked to speak to the manager on a matter of vital importance.

Once the man heard it was Signor di Malatesta investigating a possible police matter to do with the bank, he told him her last name was Peterson, and that she was from Newburgh, New York. Leon didn't often use his name to apply pressure, but this case was an exception.

He learned she'd made the reservation nearly two weeks ago and had rented the car for seven days. It seemed she'd already been in Rimini three days.

Leon thanked the manager for his cooperation. Pleased to be armed with this much information before confronting her, he made a search on his phone. Newburgh was a town sixty miles north of New York City. What it all meant he didn't know yet, but he was about to find out.

He saw the rental car when he drove down the alley and parked. Ruggio met him at the front desk of the pension, where Rosa was helping a scruffy-looking male wearing a backpack and short shorts.

"She's been in her room since she came in. She's *molta molta bellissima*," Ruggio whispered. "I think I've seen her on television."

Marcello had said the same thing. "*Grazie.* I'll take it from here," Leon told him. If she was working alone or with another reporter, he planned to find out.

Once Ruggio left, he sat down. By now it was quarter after six. Without a TV, she'd probably leave again, if only to get a meal. If he had to wait too long, he'd insist Rosa go knock on Signorina Peterson's door. To pass the time, Leon phoned Simona, and was relieved to hear his little girl seemed to be over the worst of her bug.

As he was telling his housekeeper he wasn't sure what time he'd get home, a woman emerged from the alcove. Without warning, his adrenaline kicked in. Not just because she was beautiful—in fact, incredibly so. It was because there was something about her that reminded him of someone else.

She swept past him, so fast she was out the door before he was galvanized into action. After telling Simona he'd get back to her, he sprang from the chair and followed the shapely woman in the two-piece linen suit and leather sandals down the alley to her car.

He estimated she had to be five feet six. Even the way she carried herself, with a kind of unconscious grace, was appealing. Physically, Leon could find nothing wrong with her, and that bothered him, since he hadn't been able to look at another woman since Benedetta.

"Belle Peterson?"

She wheeled around, causing her gleaming hair, the color of dark mink, to swish about her shoulders. Cobalt-blue eyes fringed with black lashes flew to Leon in surprise. If she already knew who he was, she was putting on a good act of pretending otherwise.

She possessed light olive skin that needed no makeup. Her wide mouth, with its soft pink lipstick, had a voluptuous flare. He found her the embodiment of feminine pulchritude, but to his surprise she stared at him without a hint of recognition or flirtatiousness. "How do you know my name? We've never met."

With that accent, she was American through and through. He found her directness as intriguing as her no-nonsense demeanor. Some men might find it intimidating. Leon's gaze dropped to her left hand, curled over her shoulder bag and resting against the lush curve of her hip. Her nails were well manicured with a neutral coating. She wore no rings.

If in disguise for a part she was playing—perhaps in the hope of infiltrating their family business in some way to unlock secrets—he would say she looked...perfect.

He pulled the note Berto had given him out of his suit jacket pocket and handed it to her.

She glanced at it before eyeing him again. "Evidently you're from the bank. How did you get my last name?"

"A simple matter of checking with the car rental agency."

Her blue eyes turned frosty. "I don't know about your country, but in mine that information can only be obtained by a judge's warrant during the investigation of a crime."

"My country has similar laws."

"Was it a crime to ask questions?"

"Of course not. But I'm afraid our doors are closed to all so-called journalists. I decided to investigate."

"I'm not a journalist or anything close," she stated promptly. Reaching in her shoulder bag, she pulled a business card out of her wallet.

He took it from her fingers and glanced at it. *Belle Peterson, Manager, Trans Continental Cell Phones Incorporated, Newburgh, New York...*

He lifted his head. "Why didn't you leave

this card at the bank with the security man you talked to?"

Without hesitation, she said, "Because a call to my work verifying my employment would let everyone know where I am. Since my whereabouts are no one's business, I wish it to remain that way. The fact is, I'm on vacation and it's almost over."

He slipped the card into his pocket. "You'll be returning to Newburgh?"

"Yes. I've talked to as many people with the last name Donatello as I've been able to locate in Rimini. So far I haven't found the information I've been seeking."

"Or a missing person, maybe?" he prodded. "A man, perhaps?" The question slipped out, once again surprising him. As if he cared who she was looking for...

Her gaze never wavered. "I suppose that's a natural assumption a man might make, but the answer is no. Not every woman is looking for a man, whether it be for pleasure or for marriage...an institution that in my opinion is overvaunted."

She sounded like Leon, only in reverse, increasing his interest.

"To be specific, the manager at Donatello Diamonds directed me to the Malatesta Bank, but it seems I've come to a dead end there, too. Since you prefer not to tell me your name, at least let me thank you for the courtesy of coming to the pension to let me know you can't help me. I can cross Donatello Diamonds off my list of possibilities."

Like a man concluding a business meeting, she put out her hand for Leon to shake. His closed around hers. Unexpected warmth shot up his arm, catching him off guard before he released her. "What will you do now?"

"I'll continue to search until my time runs out in three days. Goodbye." She turned and got in her rental car without asking him for the card back. He watched until she drove to the end of the alley and turned onto the street.

Her card burned a hole in his pocket. He pulled it out. If he phoned the number on the back of it, he'd find out if she'd been telling the truth about her job. But since he was a person who always jealously guarded his own privacy, he could relate to her desire to keep her private life to herself.

No matter what, this woman meant *nothing* to him. If she'd come on a fishing expedition, he hadn't given her any information she could use to cause trouble.

By the time he'd driven back to the villa, his thoughts were on his daughter. It wasn't until later, after he'd kissed her good-night and was doing laps in the pool, that images of the American woman kept surfacing. There was something familiar about her that wouldn't leave him alone.

A nagging voice urged him to phone the head office of TCCPI, wherever it was located, to find out if she'd fabricated an elaborate lie including a business card. Leon could do that before he went to bed. If he didn't make the call, he'd never get to sleep.

# CHAPTER TWO

EARLY WEDNESDAY MORNING, Belle came awake after a restless night. The tall nameless man in the light blue silk suit who'd tracked her down in the alley last evening was without question the most dangerously striking male she'd ever met in her life.

With those aquiline features, he embodied much more than the conventional traits one normally attributed to a gorgeous man, such as handsome, dashing or exciting. She couldn't believe it, but she'd been attracted to him. Strongly attracted. It had never happened to her before.

Once he'd called out to her, she'd felt his powerful presence before she'd even turned to study his rock-hard physique. His black hair and olive skin provided the perfect foil for startling gray eyes.

For him to come from the bank armed with information no one could have known meant he was someone of importance. The fact that her inquiry had brought him to the pension convinced her she'd unwittingly trespassed on ground whose secrets were so dark, they had to be well guarded.

Who better than the man who'd suddenly appeared like some mysterious prince from this Renaissance city? Just remembering their encounter sent a shiver down the length of her body.

She was being fanciful, but couldn't help it. His deep voice with barely a trace of accent in English had agitated her nervous system. Even after twelve hours she could still feel it resonating. Though she'd never forget him, she needed to push thoughts of him to the back of her mind. Her flight home Sunday would be here before she knew it, which meant she needed to intensify her search.

Once she'd showered down the hall, and had slipped on a short-sleeved, belted white cotton dress, she left the pension armed with her detailed street map and notebook. She'd kept a log of every Donatello name so far. Her destination for the last Donatello she could find in the city of Rimini was Donatello's Garage.

After following the directions she'd been given on the phone yesterday, she talked to the manager, who spoke passable English. He told her a man by another name now owned the shop. The original owner, Mr. Donatello, and his wife had both died of old age. They'd had no children who could inherit the garage.

This was the way it had been going since last Sunday, when she'd started working through the list of Donatellos in the Rimini phone directory. In most cases the people she'd talked to were willing to help her, even going to the trouble of finding someone to help them understand her English.

They were proud of their genealogy. Many of them told her she could come by their house. The others told her their information over the phone, but so far there were no leads on a woman with the middle or last name Donatello, in her late thirties or early forties, who'd been to New York twenty-six years ago. It was like looking for a needle in the proverbial haystack.

Resolving not to be dispirited, Belle thanked him and headed for the library near her pension, to do more research on the other nineteen cities and towns within Rimini Province. They were ten to twelve miles apart and had much smaller populations, so there wouldn't be as many Donatellos to look up. That could be bad, if nothing was discovered about her birth mother.

En route to the library, Belle stopped at a trattoria for breakfast and filled up so she wouldn't have to eat until dinnertime. She would be doing a lot more driving over the next few days. Before she left Rimini, she approached the woman in the research department, who spoke excellent English and knew she was looking for Donatello names.

"I have one more question, if you don't mind. Could you tell me anything about the Malatesta Bank?" The striking Italian who'd shown up at the pension had refused to leave her mind.

"How much time do you have?"

That's what Belle had thought. "Yesterday the manager of Donatello Diamonds directed me to the bank to get information, but I learned nothing. Why would he do that? I don't understand the connection."

"The House of Malatesta was an Italian family that ruled over Rimini from 1300 to 1500. There's too much history since then to tell you in five minutes. But today a member of that old ruling family, Count Sullisto Malatesta, runs the Malatesta Bank, one of the two largest banks in Italy. They own many other businesses as well.

"Another, lesser ruling family of the past, the House of Donatello, made their fortune in diamonds, but over years of poor management it started to dwindle. Some say it would have eventually failed if Count Malatesta, then a widower, hadn't merged with the House of Donatello.

"He saved it from ruin by marrying Princess Luciana Donatello, the heiress, whose father was purported to have died of natural causes." The woman lowered her voice. "I say *purported* because some people insisted both he and his wife had been murdered, either by another faction of the Donatello family, or by the Malatesta family. Soon thereafter, the count made his power grab by marrying her, but nothing definite came of the investigation to prove or disprove the theories."

Belle shuddered. The dark stranger from the bank had looked that dangerous to her.

"The Donatello deaths left a question mark and turned everything into a scandal that rocked the region and made the wedding into a nationwide event."

"You're a fount of knowledge, and I'm indebted to you," Belle told her. "Now I'm off to the other towns in Rimini Province to look up more Donatellos. Thank you so much for your time."

The woman smiled. "Good luck to you."

Belle was glad to be leaving the city, to be leaving *him*. Before she left, she would pay her bill at the pension and turn in her rental car. In case the man from the bank made more inquiries about her, he'd be thrown off the scent. Leaving no trail, she'd take a taxi to another rental agency and procure a car for the rest of the week.

She left the library and walked out to the parking lot to get in her car. As she opened the door, she heard a deep familiar voice say, "Signorina Peterson?" Her heart jumped.

It was déjà vu as she looked around and discovered the man who'd been responsible for her restless night. This time he was dressed in a blue sport shirt that made him even more breathtaking, if that was possible. His eyes played over her with a thoroughness that was disarming.

"Why are you following me, *signore?*"

"Because I overheard your conversation with the librarian and am in a position to help you in your search if you'd allow me."

"Why would you do that, when you won't even tell me your name?"

"Because you're a foreigner who has suffered two frights. The first from me, because I put you through an inquisition yesterday. The second from the librarian, who increased your nervousness just now when she answered your question."

He'd been listening the whole time? That meant he'd followed her from the pension. Belle held on to the door handle for support. "What makes you think I'm nervous?"

"The pulse in your throat is throbbing unnaturally fast."

Those silvery eyes didn't miss a detail. "I imagine it always does that when I'm being stalked."

"With your kind of beauty, I would imagine it's an occupational hazard, especially at your workplace." While she tried to catch her breath, he said, "I had you investigated."

"I knew it," she muttered.

He cocked his dark head. "Not in a way that anyone from your store could ever find out. I called headquarters in New York and explained our bank was doing the groundwork to sponsor an American cell phone company in Rimini, to see how it would play out."

"That was a lie!"

"Not necessarily. American cell phone companies are one asset we've had an idea to acquire for some time. When I asked which store manager might be equal to the task, you were mentioned among the top five managers for your company on the East Coast."

"What did you do? Talk to the CEO himself?" she demanded.

"Actually, I did."

*Good heavens.* He was handsome as the devil and just as cunning.

"I find it even more compelling that you started with that company at age eighteen and six years later are still with them. That kind of loyalty is rare. I was told you're going to be promoted to a regional manager in the next few months. Perhaps it might land you in Rimini."

*What?*

"My congratulations."

Who was this man with such powerful connections? Belle needed to keep her wits. "Just so you know, I have no interest in moving overseas. So now that you've learned I'm not one of the paparazzi, I'd like your word that you'll leave me alone, whoever you are."

"I'm Leonardo di Malatesta, the elder son of Count Sullisto Malatesta."

Her heart thudded too fast. It all fit with her first impression of a dark prince, and explained the signet ring with a knight's head on his right hand. There was a wedding ring on his left. "I understand that name connotes someone sinister."

His smile had a dangerous curl. "If it would make you feel more comfortable, call me Leon."

"The lion. If that's supposed to make me feel any better…"

A velvety sound close to a chuckle escaped his lips. "I want to apologize for my unorthodox method of getting to know you, and frightening you. Considering the fact that you plan to return to the States on Sunday, perhaps if you told me exactly what you're hoping to find, I could help speed up the process. I really would like to assist you."

"I doubt your wife would approve."

Those gray eyes darkened with some unnamed emotion. "I'm a widower."

"Yet you still wear your wedding ring. You must have loved her a great deal. Forgive me if I'm being suspicious. The truth is, I wouldn't dream of bothering a busy man like you, one with so many banking responsibilities. The only thing I was hoping to get from the manager at Donatello Diamonds was a little information about the female members of the Donatello family. It would take just a few minutes."

"So you're looking for a woman…"

"That's very astute of you."

A gleam entered his eyes. "Considering the very attractive female I'm talking to, surely I can be forgiven for my earlier assessment of the situation."

*Don't let that fatal charm of his get to you, Belle, even if he is still in mourning.*

"That depends on what you can tell me," she retorted with a wry smile back at him.

After a pause, he said, "Obviously you haven't found her yet. Why is she so important to you that you would come thousands of miles?"

The small moment of levity fled. "Because the answer to my whole existence is tied up with her. My greatest fear is that she's no longer alive, or that I'll never find her." Sorrow weighed Belle down at the thought.

He studied her with relentless scrutiny. "Is she a relative?"

This was where things got too sensitive. "Maybe."

"How old would she be?"

"Probably in her forties." Again, maybe. According to Cliff, her adoptive father had called her mother "that Italian girl." Belle took it to mean she was young. "I learned she was from Rimini, Italy, but that could mean the city or the province."

His black eyebrows furrowed. "My step-mother, Luciana, was an only child, born to Valeria and Massimo Donatello here in Rimini. Valeria died in a hunting accident on their estate when Luciana was only eleven. As the librarian told you, some people still believe it wasn't an accident."

"What she told me sounded positively Machiavellian."

"You're right. It was only a few months ago that the police finally solved the case. The shooting was ruled as accidental."

"I see. It's still tragic when any child loses its mother."

"I couldn't agree more," he said in an almost haunted voice. Their eyes held for a moment. "My father was fifteen years older than Luciana, and he married her against my brother's and my wishes. She was only twenty at the time and could never have replaced our mother."

Four years younger than Belle's age now. "Of course not." She could only imagine this man's pain. Suddenly he'd become more human to her. He'd lost his own mother and his wife.

"She's forty-two now," Leon added. "There

must be quite a few Donatello women between those ages you've met while you've been here in Rimini."

"Yes, but so far I've had no luck, because none of them ever traveled to New York in their late teens or twenties."

Leon's heart gave a thunderclap. "New York is the connecting point?" he rasped.

Belle nodded.

What had she said in answer to his earlier question about why this was important to her? *Because the answer to my whole existence is tied up with her. My greatest fear is that she's no longer alive, or that I'll never find her.*

As Leon stared at Belle, pure revelation flowed through him. He *knew* why she looked familiar to him. Had Marcello picked up on the resemblance? Or the manager at Donatello Diamonds? Probably not, or they would have said something, but he couldn't be sure. Ruggio thought he'd seen her on television.

*Madonna mia!*

"I told you I'd like to help you, and I will, but we can't talk here. Leave your car in the library parking lot and come with me. It will be safe."

"I don't need your help. Thanks all the same."

She opened her shoulder bag to get her keys, but he put a hand on her arm. "If you want to meet your mother, I'm the person who can make it happen. But you're going to have to trust me."

Her gasp told him everything he wanted to know. Those fabulous blue eyes were blurry with tears as they lifted to his. "Are you saying what I think you're saying?" Her voice shook.

"Let's find out. Is there anything in your car you need?"

"No."

"Then we'll drive to my villa, where we can talk in private. I have some pictures to show you."

She moved like a person in a daze as he escorted her to his car and helped her inside. At a time like this, the shape of her long, elegant legs shouldn't have drawn his attention, but they did. Her flowery fragrance proved another assault on his senses.

"Do I look like her?"

"When I saw you come out of the alcove at the pension yesterday, you reminded me of someone, but I couldn't place you. It's bothered me ever since. Not until a few minutes ago, when you mentioned New York, did everything click into place." He started the engine. "You'll need to buckle up."

Leon wove through the streets to the villa, not really seeing anything while his mind played back through the years to the time he'd first met Luciana. He remembered his father telling him and Dante that she'd lived in New York for a year and could help them improve their English. How much had his parent known about the sober young princess he'd brought home to the palazzo, besides the fact that she had money and was beautiful?

Yet even if she'd told him nothing about having a baby, his father would have guessed, if she'd had a C-section or stretch marks. If not, he might still be in the dark. Her terrible secret might explain why she'd always seemed so remote and elusive to Leon.

Before they reached the house he phoned Simona. After learning Concetta was back to normal and playing with her new buckets in the kitchen, he told his housekeeper to prepare lunch for him and a guest. They'd be arriving shortly and could eat out on the patio.

Engrossed in her own thoughts, the woman seated next to him hadn't said a word during the drive. Once upon a time she'd been a baby, separated at birth from her mother by an ocean. When Leon thought about his little daughter and how precious she was to him, he couldn't fathom Belle's or Luciana's history. Leon had so many questions he didn't know which one to ask first.

When the white, two-story villa built along neoclassic lines came into view, he pressed the remote to open the gates and drove around to the back. When she saw the flower garden there, Belle gave a gasp of admiration.

Leon helped her from the car and led her up the steps into the rear foyer that opened into the dayroom. "At the end of the hallway is a guest bedroom with bath, where you can freshen up. When you're ready, come and find me in here, and we'll eat lunch on the patio, where we won't be disturbed."

"Thank you."

The second she disappeared, he hurried through the main floor to the kitchen, where he found Concetta in her playpen with some toys. She made delighted sounds when she saw him, and lifted her arms. He gathered her up and kissed her half a dozen times against her neck, causing her to laugh. Again he was reminded that his lunch guest had never known her mother's kiss. Obviously not her father's, either.

Talia smiled. "She's had her lunch and is ready for her nap."

"I brought company, so I can't give her all my attention, but I will when she wakes up." He kissed her once more and handed her back to Talia. His daughter didn't like being separated from him, and shed a few tears going down the hall to the staircase.

Much as he wanted to put her to bed himself, he was aware someone else was waiting for him, someone who'd been waiting years for any word about her parentage.

Simona looked over her shoulder. "Do you want lunch served now?"

"Please."

He retraced his steps to the dayroom and found Belle holding a five-by-seven framed photo she'd picked up from a grouping on one of the credenzas. Her back was turned to him, but even from this distance, he could see her shoulders shaking.

"I won't pretend to say I understand what you're feeling. I can only imagine what it must be like to see yourself in Luciana's image. Though you're not identical, anyone who knows you well would notice certain similarities."

Belle put the picture back and whirled around, her lovely face dripping with tears.

She used both hands to wipe them off her chin. "My mother is a princess? *Your* step-mother? I—I can't take it in," she stammered. "In the orphanage I used to dream about what she would be like. I had to believe she gave me up because of a life-and-death reason. But my dreams never reached heights like that."

Leon put his hands on his hips. "I'm still in shock from the knowledge that she had a baby, yet there's never been a whisper of you."

He heard his guest groan. "When Cliff told me my mother was from Italy, I wanted it to be the truth. But I never thought I'd really find her. Why did you bother to come to the pension?" The throb in her voice hung in the air.

It was the question Leon had been asking himself over and over. He rubbed the back of his neck. "I can't honestly tell you the reason. It was a feeling that nagged at me to the point I had to investigate."

She clasped her hands together. "If you hadn't come, I would know *nothing,* and I would be flying back to New York without ever getting an answer. Thank heaven for you!" she cried. "I'll never be able to repay you."

A strange shiver chased through his body at the realization he might not have heeded the prompting. He'd tried to ignore it, until he'd been swimming in the pool. Then it wouldn't leave him alone.

Belle's gorgeous eyes searched his. "But now that I see her picture, I think I'm frightened. It's like that old expression about being careful what you wish for, because you might get it."

She wasn't the only one alarmed. Already she was important to him in ways he couldn't begin to explain.

"Is it because you've discovered you're the stepsister through marriage of the infamous Malatesta family?"

He'd thrown the question at her in a silky voice to combat her pull on him. His attraction to her was sucking him in deeper and deeper. He didn't want this kind of complication in his life, not after having lost Benedetta. Too many losses convinced him it was better not to get involved. Leon had his daughter. She was all he needed.

His guest stared at him through haunted eyes. "What are you talking about? When the couple who adopted me brought me to their house, they broke their birth son's heart. He hated me from the first day. If anything,

I'm afraid of being the orphaned offspring of the woman your father brought into your home, thereby breaking *your* heart."

Her words touched on Leon's deep-seated guilt, and confounded him. She really was frightened. He could feel it. "You're pale and need to eat. Come out to the patio with me."

Leon showed her though the tall French doors on the far side of the dayroom. Simona had set the round, wrought-iron table with a cloth and fresh flowers from the garden. She'd prepared bruschetta and her *bocconcini* salad of mozzarella balls and *cubetti di pancetta* ham he particularly enjoyed.

He helped Belle to a seat where she could look out at the Adriatic. With the hot, fair weather, he spotted half a dozen sailboats and a few yachts out on the water. It was a sight he never tired of, especially now with the view of her alluring profile filling his vision.

Once he'd poured her some iced tea he said, "If you'd prefer coffee or juice, I'll ask Simona to bring it."

But Belle had already taken a long swallow. "This tastes delicious and is exactly what I needed. Thank you."

After drinking half a glass himself, he

picked up his fork and they started to eat. "I'm assuming Cliff is the son you referred to."

She nodded. "The Petersons adopted me when I was ten. Mr. Peterson never wanted me, but Nadine had always hoped for a daughter and finally prevailed on him to adopt me. They already had a sixteen-year-old son, who had no desire for a girl from an orphanage to move in on what he considered his territory."

Leon's stomach muscles clenched in reaction. He could relate to Cliff's hatred at that age. Leon had been eleven when his father had installed the twenty-year-old Luciana in the palazzo, a world that had belonged to him and his brother, Dante. *No one else.*

Now that the years had passed, and Leon had his own home and was a father, he understood better his parent's need for companionship. At eleven he'd been too selfish to see anything beyond his own wants.

From the beginning he'd rebuffed any overtures from Luciana, but he had to admit she'd never been unkind to him or Dante. Anything but. As the years went by, he'd learned to be more civil to her. Maturity helped him to see that her cool aloofness at times masked some kind of strange sadness, no doubt because she'd lost both her parents under tragic circumstances.

To think she'd had a baby she'd been forced to give up! The knowledge tore him apart inside. He could never give up Concetta for any reason.

"How did it happen that Cliff told you about your mother?"

After putting her fork down, Belle told him what had transpired at the attorney's office. Leon was astounded by what he heard. For her adoptive brother to take the money before telling her what she'd been desperate to know all her life sickened Leon. What made Cliff more despicable to him was to learn he hadn't let her keep the money that was legally hers.

"Tell me about your life with the Petersons. I'd like to hear."

She looked at him for a minute as if testing his sincerity. Then she began in a halting voice. "The day I was taken to their house, Cliff followed me into the small room that would be my bedroom. He grabbed me by the shoulders and told me his dad hadn't wanted a screaming baby around the house. That's why they'd picked me. But I'd better be good and stay out of his dad's way or I'd be sorry, Cliff said. And in fact his father was so intimidating, I tried hard to be obedient and not cause trouble."

Leon grimaced. "They should never have been allowed to adopt you."

"Laws weren't so strict then. The orphanage was overcrowded. You know how it is."

As far as Leon was concerned, it was criminal.

"Ben was a car salesman who loved old cars and had restored several, but it took all their money. He lost his job several times because of layoffs, and had to find employment at other car dealerships. The money he poured into his hobby ate up any extra funds they had. He was an angry man who never had a kind word. The more I tried to gain his favor, the more he dismissed me."

*And destroyed her confidence,* Leon bet.

"Nadine held a job at a dry cleaners and was a hard worker who tried to make a good home for us. She took me to church. It was one of the few places where I found comfort. But she was a quiet woman unable to show affection. It was clear she was afraid of her own son and stayed out of her husband's way as much as possible. I never bonded with any of them."

"How could you have under those circumstances?" Leon was troubled by her story.

"One good thing happened to me. As soon as I was old enough, I did babysitting for people in the neighborhood to earn money. I'd helped out with the younger children in the orphanage and knew how to play with them and care for babies. I love them." Her voice trembled.

There was a sweetness in Belle that got under his skin.

"To tell you the truth, I liked going to other people's houses to get away from Cliff and his father, who were so mean-spirited. He constantly asked me for money, telling me he'd pay me back, but he never did. I didn't tell on him for fear Ben would take out his anger on me."

With each revelation Leon's hands curled into tighter fists.

"Finally Cliff got a job in a garage after school, and in time bought himself a motorcycle. That kept him away from me, but from then on it seemed he was always in trouble with traffic tickets and accidents.

"He was often at odds with both his parents because of the hours he kept with girls they didn't know. Sometimes he barged into my room, to take out his frustration on me by bullying me. He never lost an opportunity to let me know I'd ruined his life," she whispered.

"I can't begin to imagine how you made it through those hellish years, Belle."

"When I look back on it neither can I. The day I turned eighteen, I got a job in a cell phone store and moved in with three others girls, sharing an apartment. It saved my life to get away from my nightmarish situation."

"Did Cliff follow you?"

"No. I left while he was gone. He had no idea where I went, and could no longer come after me for money and badger me. The few times I went to see Nadine, I went by her work at the dry cleaners so Cliff never saw me. She knew things were out of control with him and never pushed for me to come home again, because I was over the legal age."

Certain things Belle had just said brought home to Leon how mean-spirited he'd been to Luciana when she'd first come to live at the palazzo. He'd been an adolescent and had ignored any overtures on her part. Dante had done the same thing to her, following in his big brother's footsteps.

"I only ever saw him at the church funeral and the attorney's office after that," Belle explained. "When he told me my last name, I didn't know if it was the truth. But I wanted it to be true, so badly that I flew to Rimini on a prayer, knowing I'd seen the last of him, and was thankful."

Shaken by her revelations, Leon wiped the corner of his mouth with a napkin. "You didn't learn anything about your birth father through Cliff?"

She drank the last of her tea. "No. I decided he must have disappeared before my mother took me to the orphanage. What other explanation could there be...unless something horrendous had happened and she'd been raped? I shudder to think that might have been the case, and would rather not talk about it."

"Then we won't." If Luciana had been raped, and Leon's father knew about it, how would he feel about Belle, the innocent second victim? The more Leon thought about it, the more it was like a bomb exploding, the resulting shock waves wreaking devastation. "What's the name of the orphanage?"

"The Newburgh Church Orphanage. Why do you ask?"

He put down his fork. "Despite the public's opinion of the Malatesta family, we give to a number of charities. Your story has decided me to send an anonymous donation to the orphanage where you were raised.

That's something I intend to take care of right away."

A gift no matter how large wouldn't take away his guilt over his treatment of Luciana, but he realized the only reason Belle was still alive was due to the generosity of others who gave to charity.

"If you did that, the sisters would consider it heaven sent, but you don't need to do it."

"I want to. They gave you a spiritual and physical start in life. No payment would be enough."

"You're right," she said in a quiet voice. "One of the sisters in charge reminded us that we were lucky to be there where we could get the help we needed, so we shouldn't complain. The priest at the church where Nadine took me told me I was blessed to have a birth mother who loved me enough to put me in God's keeping."

Hard words for a child to accept, but Leon could only agree. Whatever Luciana's circumstances at the time, she'd at least had the courage to make certain her baby would be looked after. His admiration for her choice when she could have done something else changed his perception of her. But why had she given up her baby?

Had Luciana loved that baby with all her

heart, the way he'd loved Concetta from the moment he'd learned they were expecting? He knew enough about Luciana's strict upbringing to realize she would have been afraid of letting anyone find out about her baby, causing a scandal that would tarnish the Donatello family name.

Unbelievable that her offspring had grown up into a beautiful, intelligent woman eating lunch with *him,* no less! *You're enjoying it far too much, Malatesta.*

Luciana had lived through a nightmare, and had gone on to make a home for his father and the boys despite Leon's antipathy. An unfamiliar sense of shame for his behavior over those early years crept into his psyche. He was now paying the price.

"Their goodness to you needs to be rewarded," he murmured, still trying to digest everything.

"Sometimes I felt guilty for wanting to know about my parents when the sisters tried so hard to keep our spirits up. When Cliff asked me why I wanted to find someone who didn't want me, I told him it wasn't important if they didn't want me. I just needed to know who I am and where I came from. But I'm not your responsibility, and I've taken up too much of your time as it is."

She pushed herself away from the table and stood up. "Now that I have answers to those questions, I can go back to New York. Needless to say, I'll be indebted to you for the rest of my life. Thank you for bringing me to your villa, and please thank the cook for the wonderful food. If you'll drive me back to the library, I'd be very grateful."

Leon got to his feet. "We haven't even scratched the surface yet."

"Yes, we have. You and I both know there are reasons why she gave me up. I would never want to cause her pain by showing up uninvited and unwanted."

"You could never be unwanted!" he declared. He refused to believe it, but that was the father in him speaking, the father who idolized his little girl. Ever since Belle was born, she'd never known the love of her own parents. He couldn't fathom it.

# CHAPTER THREE

"You say that with such fervency, Leon, but we know the facts, don't we. My mother came back to Italy and married your father. Unless you're aware of other information, I'm sure she has never tried to find me."

"I have no idea and neither do you. Nevertheless—"

"Nevertheless, she and your father have made a life for themselves," Belle interrupted. "Last year I went to the orphanage for a final time to beg them to tell me something about my roots. I had a talk with the sister in charge." The tremor in Belle's voice penetrated to Leon's insides.

"What did she say to you?"

"She told me she wasn't at liberty to tell me anything, because my adoption was a closed case. Then she handed me a pamphlet to read. It was called 'A Practical Guide for the Adopted Child.' The material was based on research gathered by the psychiatric community. She said we'd discuss it after I'd finished it."

"And did you?"

"Yes!" she cried. "The whole brochure described me so perfectly, I went into shock."

"Explain what you mean."

She moistened her lips nervously. "I've always had issues of self-esteem. Not to know who you are because you were given up for adoption means you don't have an identity. All my life I've wanted to know if I looked like my birth parents, or acted like them.

"What if I had sisters and brothers I knew nothing about? What if I came from a large family with half siblings or extended family I would never meet or get to know? It used to drive me crazy, wondering."

"Belle...at least now you know you have a mother and a stepfamily who are very much alive."

"Yes," she whispered, staring blindly out to sea. "If I do meet her I'll be able to learn about my birth father. I longed for a father, too, and spent many hours daydreaming about him. But I'm terrified, Leon, because I *was* abandoned. Being abandonable meant I wasn't good enough to be kept and loved. That's a very hard thing to accept."

What she was telling Leon made him sick inside. "Since you don't know the circumstances of being left at the orphanage, don't you realize your adoptive father and brother have contributed to a lot of those negative feelings?"

"Of course." She took a shaky breath. "But to meet my own birth mother after all this time and find out from her own lips I hadn't been loved or wanted would shatter me. I don't know if I could handle it. The risk is too great."

Leon shook his head. "That's not going to happen to you. If you could see the loving way Luciana treats people..." Luciana was very loving to his daughter when he took Concetta over for visits. "You would see that your mother has an innate tenderness that goes soul deep." Leon had seen and felt it, but in the beginning he hadn't wanted to acknowledge it.

"Even so, I know I'm setting myself up to learn that everything I've ever thought or dreamed of about her and my father won't be as I assumed. You've told me she hasn't had other children, but she's a princess who has lived a life completely different from mine in every way, shape and form. The chances of her even wanting to meet the daughter she gave up are astronomical."

"That's not true. You don't know her as I do."

"I know you want to believe she'll be happy to see me, but you can't know what's deep in her heart. And there's your father to consider. The more I know about her and their life, the more I fear a permanent reunion could never be realized."

"It's true I don't know her inner thoughts." Leon's mind reeled when he compared the two women's worlds. And he had no idea how his father would react upon hearing the news that Luciana's daughter was in Rimini.

"Even if she's willing to meet me, how will she handle it? She thought she gave me up and would never see me again. Even if meeting me could satisfy the question of what happened to me, it wouldn't solve the issues she had for giving me up in the first place.

"What if seeing me exacerbates problems that bring new heartache?" Belle sounded frantic. "This meeting might result in trouble between her and your father, and they'll wish this had never happened…"

She wheeled around, her face white as parchment. Tears glistened like diamonds on those pale cheeks. "What if I brought on a crisis like that?"

Tortured by the fear and pain in her voice, Leon reached for her and rocked her in his arms like he would Concetta when she was upset and frightened. "Shhh. That's not going to happen, Belle. I swear it." He kissed her hair and forehead without thinking.

"I—I don't want it to happen, but you can't guarantee anything."

Much as Leon hated to admit it, everything she'd revealed from her heart and soul made a hell of a lot of sense. But suddenly he had other things on his mind. When he'd pulled her to him, his only thought had been to comfort her. Yet the feel of her curves against his body invaded his senses, sending a quickening through him, one so powerful he needed to put her away from him. As gently as he could, he let go of her.

Belle took a step back before looking up at him through red-rimmed eyes. "The sister warned me my time would be better served by getting on with my own life rather than wasting it trying to find my birth mother, who obviously didn't want to be found.

"I left the orphanage with the renewed resolve to get on with my career and put my dreams away. Then came the moment in the attorney's office when Cliff made that slip about my birth mother being Italian."

"A providential slip, in my opinion," Leon muttered. He was beginning to believe some unseen power had been at work on both sides of the Atlantic. Otherwise how could he account for going to her pension to talk to her, when normally he would have left it alone?

"I agree, Leon. The second it happened, I ignored the sister's warning and the words in the pamphlet. I thought I knew better, and left for Italy, determined to keep looking. Now I wish I'd listened to her."

To his consternation, Leon was thankful she hadn't obeyed the sister in charge.

Belle's pleading eyes trapped his. "My mother's secrets are safe with me, and they have to remain safe with you, Leon. They *have* to." The desperation in her voice pulled on his chaotic emotions.

"They'll be safe as long as you do something important for me."

"What?" Her breathing came in spurts.

"I insist you stay in my house as my guest until you return to the States. If you don't let me do anything else, at least accept my hospitality. Our parents are married. That one fact bonds us in a way you can't deny."

"I wasn't going to, but since I got the in-

formation I came for, I'm planning to fly
back to New York either tonight or in the
morning. Every second I'm here, it's worse.
The possibility that she could find out I'm a
guest in your villa terrifies me. Whether she
wanted me or not doesn't matter. She gave
me life and I'd rather die than hurt her."

Leon's admiration for Belle grew in quan-
tum leaps. "I believe you would," he murmured, before making a quick decision.
"Your mind appears made up, so I'll see you
back to your rental car."

"Thank you."

"I'll meet you in the foyer after I let my
housekeeper know I'm leaving."

She nodded, and he went to find Simona.
On his way back through the house he
stopped in the dayroom to pick up the photograph Belle had been looking at. It showed
Luciana and his father on their wedding day,
outside the church. At twenty she bore an
even stronger resemblance to her daughter.

When he reached the foyer, he found Belle
studying a large oil painting of his family. "That's my brother leaning against my
mother."

"You look about six years old there. How
old was Dante?"

"Five. We're just fourteen months apart."

She turned to him. "What a handsome family. You resemble both your parents."

"Genes don't lie, do they?"

"No. Your mother has the most wonderful smile."

"She was the most wonderful everything."

Belle stared at him. "You were very lucky to have a mother like that. What was her name?"

"Regina Emilia of the House of Della Rovere in Pesaro."

"A princess?"

"Yes." He opened the door so she could walk past him. After he helped her into the car, he handed her the photograph. "I want you to have this. No one deserves it more than you do."

Tears sprang to Belle's eyes. "I couldn't take it."

"There are dozens more where this came from." He shut the door and walked around to get behind the wheel.

Belle was still incredulous over what had happened. She hugged the photograph to her chest in wonder that she'd come to the end of her search. It was all because of Leon Malatesta, who was the most remarkable man she'd ever met. But it wasn't his generosity that had caused her to tremble in his arms just now.

While he'd been holding her, kissing her like he would to comfort a child, feelings of a different kind had curled through her like flame. The need to taste his mouth and let go of her feelings had grown so intense, she knew she was in deep trouble. He was her *stepbrother!*

In the past, when her friends had talked about desire, she'd never experienced it. Until a few minutes ago she hadn't known what it felt like. Shame washed over her to think she hadn't wanted him to stop what he was doing to her. By easing away from her before she was ready, he'd sent her into another kind of shock.

"Are you all right, Belle?"

"Yes. I—I'm just feeling overwhelmed," she stammered.

"Who could blame you?"

If he knew her intimate thoughts, he'd drive her straight to the airport right now. Earlier, he'd been ready to run her out of town, when he'd thought she was some gutter reporter out to dig up something salacious about his family. Instead he'd come after her at the pension and had single-handedly led her to her dream of finding her mother.

To tell him she was indebted to him couldn't begin to convey what was in her heart. To think that after all these years of aching to know anything about her origins she had her answer...

With one glance at the amazing man behind the wheel, Belle knew she could trust him to keep his silence. It was herself she didn't trust. There was such a huge part of her that wanted to visit her mother while she was still in Rimini; it was killing her.

The sooner Belle left Italy the better. But that meant she'd never see Leon again. How would she stand it?

*You* have *to handle it, Belle.*

Before they reached the library, she put the picture in her shoulder bag and pulled out her car keys. The minute he turned into the parking space next to her rental, she opened the door and got out, before he could help her. It only took a moment before she was ensconced in her own vehicle and ready to drive off.

As his tall, powerful frame approached, she opened the window. "Thank you for everything, Leon. I'll never forget your kindness or the photograph."

"I'll never forget *you,*" he said in his deep

voice. "Good luck in your future position at TCCPI. Have a safe trip home."

*Home*. The word didn't have the same meaning anymore. "Goodbye." She started the engine and drove out to the main street. As soon as she reached the pension, she would phone to change her flight plans.

Through the rearview mirror she could see Leon standing there watching her, a bold, dynamic throwback from an earlier time in Italian history.

When she turned the corner and he was no longer in sight, a troubling thought came to her. He'd given her no grief about leaving Italy immediately. Her heart jumped all over the place because he'd made their parting far too easy. In truth, she knew the dark, mysterious son of the count could move heaven and earth if he felt like it.

Once Belle's rental car had disappeared, Leon pulled out his cell phone and gave Ruggio instructions to go to the pension and keep a close eye on her. If she went anywhere, he was to follow her.

After making a call to Simona to find out how his little girl was doing, and let his housekeeper know he might not be home until late, he headed for the bank to talk to his father. Leon found him in his suite on a business call. His parent waved him inside.

While Leon waited, he poured himself a cup of coffee from the sideboard and paced the floor with it. Whether his father knew about Belle's existence or not, what Leon had to tell him was going to come as a shock.

"It's good to see you," his father exclaimed after hanging up the phone. "Have you dropped in to tell me you're willing to consider ending your mourning period and start looking at another woman I have in mind for you?"

"No, Papà."

By marrying Benedetta, Leon had foiled his father's plan for him to marry a woman of rank he'd carefully picked out for him. The hurt hadn't been intentional, but Leon had always cared for Benedetta and refused to honor his father's wishes in the matter of his marriage. No argument the count raised had made any difference to Leon.

In that regard he wasn't so different from his widowed parent, who'd married a second time while Leon and Dante had begged him not to. But their pleading fell on deaf ears, and there'd been tension with their father ever since he'd brought Luciana into their home.

"I'm here to discuss something of a very delicate nature." Leon locked the door to his suite so no one could interrupt them. "Since I know you just passed your annual medical exam without any major problems, I feel you can handle this."

The count's dark brows met in a distinct frown. "You're beginning to make me nervous, Leonardo."

"Not as nervous as I am." He stared at his father. "This has to do with Luciana."

"Do you think she's hiding something from me since her medical exam?"

Leon heard the worry in his father's voice, revealing how much he cared about her. "I thought you told me she's as fine as you are. I'm talking about a secret she might have kept from you before you married her." Leon never was one to beat about the bush.

His last comment brought his father to his feet. Their gazes clung. *"You know?"*

The coffee cup almost fell out of Leon's hand. That one question told him his father had known about Luciana's baby all these years. He put the cup back on the sideboard. "If we're talking about a child she had out of wedlock, then yes."

Sullisto's gray eyes bordered on charcoal

and were dimmed by moisture. "How did you find out?" he asked in a shaken voice.

Leon took a fortifying breath. "Before I answer that question, just tell me one thing. Did she want to give it up, or did she have to? I need to know the absolute truth before I say another word."

A look of sorrow crossed over his father's face. "She *had* to."

"Was she raped?"

The question hung like a live wire between them.

The older man took a deep breath. "No."

"Do you know the name of the father?"

A nerve throbbed in his cheek. "Yes. But *I* wasn't the father, if that's what you're thinking."

"I wasn't thinking it," Leon replied with total honesty. "I know you're an honorable man."

"Thank you for that." The count cleared his throat. "To answer your first question, Luciana wanted her little girl more than life itself. A day doesn't go by that she's not missing her, wanting to be with her. She doesn't talk about it all the time, but even after all these years, I see the sadness and witness her tears when she doesn't know I'm aware."

Hearing those words brought such relief

to him for Belle's sake, it broke the cords binding Leon's chest. "How could she have given her up?"

"You have to hear the whole story, *figlio mio*."

"I'm listening."

His father paced the floor. "Luciana's father had many enemies and believed his wife was murdered. Afraid his daughter was in danger, he sent Luciana to a special college in New York at eighteen, under an assumed name, while he had his wife's death investigated.

"While she was away, she met a student. They fell in love and soon she found out she was expecting. Her situation became desperate because she knew her father would never agree to a marriage between them."

"But she was pregnant! Was he that tyrannical?"

"That's a harsh word, Leonardo. Let's just say he was a rigid man. Luciana and her lover decided to be married by a justice of the peace in a town an hour away from New York City, where she was in school. But on the day before the wedding could take place, he was killed in a hit-and-run accident. The driver was never apprehended."

Leon grimaced. "Luciana must have thought she was in a nightmare."

"Exactly. Because of what had happened to her mother, she was afraid she'd been hunted down and her lover murdered."

Aghast, Leon said, "When did she tell you all this?"

"When I asked her to marry me. You see, despite all the rumors about my wanting to take over the Donatello Diamonds empire, the reason I married her was because I'd learned to care for her a great deal."

"It's all right, Papà. You can call it what it was. You loved her."

"So you've guessed it."

"Yes."

His father breathed deeply. "Her sorrow was so great, I thought that having two stepsons to help raise would ease a little of her pain. You boys were only ten and eleven, and needed a mother, especially Dante." His voice trembled. "As for me, I needed someone who could share my life. Naturally, it wasn't like the feelings I had for your mother, but then, you can't expect that."

Leon couldn't believe what he was hearing. They'd never had this conversation about his mother before. Belle was the catalyst to force a discussion that should have taken place years earlier.

"Luciana's father was overjoyed, because he knew I would take care of her. Before she gave me an answer, she said she had something to tell me that no one else knew about, not even her father. If I still wanted her, then she would accept my proposal.

"I listened while it all came pouring out. After bitter anguish and soul searching, she'd felt she had no choice but to give up the baby for adoption so nothing would happen to her precious daughter.

"When she gave her up, she had to sign a paper that meant she could never see her child again or take her back. It was a sealed document. Luciana signed it because she was positive her own days were numbered, but at that point she didn't care about herself. When she returned to Rimini, she wasn't the same vivacious girl I'd known before she left."

Again Leon stood there, dumbfounded by the revelations.

"Her honesty only deepened my respect for her."

It appeared Belle had inherited that same admirable characteristic from her mother.

"Not long after our marriage, her father died of heart failure. She needed me more than ever." Sullisto eyed his son soberly. "But you still haven't answered *my* question."

Leon shook his head. "After what you've told me, I'm not sure it would be the wise thing to do."

"You don't trust me?"

"That's not it. I'm thinking of her daughter, who came to Rimini this week looking for the mother who gave her up."

*"What?"*

Leon nodded. "Sit down, Papà, while I tell you a story about Belle Peterson."

A few minutes later his father was wiping his eyes. "I can't even begin to tell you what this is going to mean to Luciana when she finds out."

"Except that Belle doesn't want Luciana to know anything." For the next few minutes he told his father what had been contained in that pamphlet, and Belle's fear of hurting her mother.

"Hurt her?" Sullisto cried out. "It would have the opposite effect! I know what I'm talking about. The one thing in our marriage that has kept us from being truly happy has been Luciana's soul-deep sadness. We tried to have a baby, but weren't successful. She's always believed God was punishing her for giving up her child."

*"Incredibile—"*

"Not until two months ago did we learn that Valeria's death was ruled accidental. That very day I begged Luciana to call the orphanage and find out what had happened to Belle. At least inquire if she'd been adopted. But she said she didn't dare, because she was afraid her daughter would hate her. I told her I'd hire a private investigator to locate her, but Luciana was convinced Belle would refuse to talk to her, after she'd given her up."

"Belle has the exact same fear, that her mother won't like her."

His father rubbed his hands together. "To know she has come all this way looking for her mother will be like a dream Luciana never thought could come true."

"Then you don't have a problem if they're united?"

"Mind? How can you even ask me that?" he cried. "It's my dream to make Luciana happy, but it has always been out of my hands."

That was all Leon needed to know. He could only imagine Belle's joy when the two of them finally met. "I have a plan. Bring

Luciana to the villa for dinner this evening.
Tell her the baby is better."

His father nodded. "She's been waiting
forever for an official invitation from you."

"I know. I'm sorry about that, but it's
something I plan to rectify."

It was regrettable, but true, that though
his father had come by the villa on occasion, Leon had never invited them over as
a couple. His cool attitude toward Luciana
had prevailed all these years. He wished he'd
known early on that she'd given up her child.
It wouldn't have changed his feelings over
his father's remarriage at the time, but he
might not have been so quick to judge her
because of false assumptions and the many
rumors that had reached his teenage ears.

"It doesn't matter, Leonardo. I know how
much your mother meant to you and Dante,
and I've understood. As for Luciana, we both
know how much she loves your Concetta and
will rejoice at the opportunity to be with her
in your home."

Leon did know that. "Come at seven. By
then Concetta will have been fed."

His father seemed more alive as they
walked to the door. He gave Leon the kind
of hug they hadn't shared in years. It wasn't
just the fact that Leon had broken down and

invited them both over for dinner. Only now was he beginning to understand how much his father had suffered in his second marriage because of Luciana's pain.

Once Leon left the bank, he alerted Simona about the plans for the evening, then drove to the pension. Ruggio was parked two cars behind Belle's rental near the entrance. Leon walked over to thank his security man, and told him he wouldn't need him any longer for surveillance.

A feeling of excitement he hadn't known in over a year passed through him as he went inside the pension and pressed the buzzer to announce his arrival. Before long Rosa appeared. *"Signore?"*

"Forgive me for not introducing myself before. My name is Leonardo di Malatesta, *signora*." The older woman's eyes widened in recognition of his name. "I need to see Signorina Peterson on a matter of life and death." He'd spoken the truth and felt no guilt about it. "I know she's here. Ask her to come out to the foyer, *per favore*." He put several bills on the counter for the woman's trouble.

After a slight hesitation she nodded and hurried through the alcove. Leon didn't have to wait long before Belle appeared, with a tear-ravaged face and puffy eyes. He wasn't surprised to see her in this kind of pain.

"Leon?" Her breathing sounded ragged. "What are you doing here? We've already said goodbye." Maybe he was crazy, but he had the gut feeling she was glad to see him.

"Yes, we did, but something's come up. Let's go to your room and I'll tell you what's happened."

She nodded. "All right." Any fight she might have put up seemed to have gone out of her for the moment.

Leon thanked Rosa before trailing Luciana's daughter into the alcove and down the hall to her small room. She was still dressed in the white dress she'd been wearing, but it looked wrinkled.

When they went inside and he'd shut the door, he saw the indention on the single bed, where she'd been sobbing. Leon knew she couldn't bear the thought of having to leave Italy without meeting her mother.

He came straight to the point. "I went to see my father after I left you."

"Oh no—"

"Before you get upset, hear me out. I learned that he knew all about you before he married your mother." Belle's eyes widened as if in disbelief. "I asked him if Luciana had wanted to give up her baby, or if she'd *had* to."

Belle's fear was palpable. "W-what did he say?"

"I'll quote you his answer. He said, 'She had to, but she wanted her little girl more than life itself. A day doesn't go by that she's not missing her, wanting to be with her.'"

Belle turned away from him to hide her emotions. Without considering the ramifications, he grasped her shoulders and turned her around to face him. Her body trembled like a leaf in the wind. Earlier when he'd held her, it hadn't been long enough. This time he drew her against him and wrapped his arms around her.

Her gleaming dark hair tickled his jaw as he murmured, "Whatever plans you've already made to fly back to New York will have to be put on hold, because he's bringing her to my villa tonight for dinner so you two can meet."

An unmistakable cry escaped Belle's lips. She tried to get away, but he wouldn't allow it, and crushed her to him. "She won't have any idea you're going to be there. My father believes this is the best way to handle it, and I do, too. He wouldn't want this if he didn't believe she'll be overjoyed. If you need more convincing, I'll phone and tell him to come over here."

Belle's head was burrowed against Leon's chest, reminding him of the way Concetta sought comfort when she was upset. He rubbed his hands over her back.

"How can you possibly leave and not see her?" he argued. "This is the opportunity you've been waiting for all your life. You've been so strong. You've survived an existence that would have defeated anyone else. Don't you realize how proud your mother's going to be of you and what you've accomplished?"

"I want to believe it."

"Would it help if I told you *I'm* proud of you? When the head of your company sang your praises, I could have told him what a remarkable woman you really are. How you survived in that household is beyond me. The methodical way you've gone about trying to find your mother in a foreign country, with no help from anyone but yourself, defies description."

He heard sniffing. "Thank you for those kind words."

*Belle...*

"I'll wait while you gather all your belongings. For the rest of the time you're in Italy, you're going to be my guest. Don't worry about your rental car. If you'll leave the key at the desk, one of my staff will return it to the agency. When we arrive at the house, you'll have the rest of the day to get ready for this evening."

"You're far too good to me."

He pressed his lips against her temple. "Why wouldn't I be? For you to find your mother with my help after all these years brings me great happiness." *It's a gift I couldn't give my daughter, but I can give it to you.* "You wouldn't deprive me of it, would you?"

Slowly she lifted her head. One corner of her lovely mouth lifted. "No. Of course not, but I'm so nervous. What if—"

"Don't go there," he interrupted in a quiet voice, kneading her upper arms. "I can promise you that if she knew what was ahead for tonight, her fear would be much greater than yours.

"Papà told me that for years she has grieved because your case was sealed when she gave you up. Even if she could get a court order for information, she's been afraid you would find it unforgivable, what she did, and would reject her out of hand."

"Is this the truth?" Fear mixed with hope in Belle's voice.

"Ask my father. He wouldn't lie to me and is excited for the two of you to meet. It can't happen soon enough for either of us."

"Then he's truly not upset?"

"Anything but. He believes this reunion will help solve certain problems in his marriage."

"What do you mean?"

"Her sadness for having to give you up, and his inability to take it away."

"Oh, Leon…" Belle's heart was in her eyes.

Unable to deny the attraction, he cupped her face in his hands, but it wasn't enough. He needed to taste her, and lowered his head, kissing her fully on the mouth. Right or wrong, she'd been a temptation from the outset.

As he coaxed her lips apart, wanting more, he drew a response from her that shot fire through him. What should have been one kiss deepened into another, then another. He should have been able to stop what was happening, but she'd aroused too much excitement in him.

"Belle…" He moaned her name, hungry for her. But in the next instant she tore her mouth from his and backed up against the door. He felt totally bereft. "Why did you pull away from me?"

"Someone has to stop this insanity!" she gasped, obviously trying to catch her breath. "I'm not blaming you. I could have resisted you, but I didn't because…I enjoyed it."

An honest woman.

"I could say I didn't know what got into me, but that would be a lie," she added. "The fact is I've never been this intimate with a man and I forgot myself."

"You're saying…"

"Shocking, isn't it? At twenty-four?" she blurted. "When I didn't try to stop you, I—I can understand why you kept kissing me. You enjoyed a happy marriage and miss your wife. As for me, I have no excuse, so let's just agree that this was a physical aberration that shouldn't have happened, and promise we'll never find ourselves in this situation again. Promise me, Leon. Otherwise I can't go through with anything, even if it means never meeting my mother." She had fire in her eyes.

"I swear I'll never do anything you don't want me to do. Does that make you feel any better?"

"No."

More astounding honesty. "While you

pack, I'll go out to the lobby and take care of the bill."

She moved away from the door. "I don't expect you to pay for me."

"I know. That's why I want to," he murmured. She didn't have a mercenary bone in her beautiful body. Just now her mouth had almost given him a heart attack. Belle Peterson had many parts to her, all of them unexpected and thrilling. After Benedetta died, he thought he'd never desire another woman.

He left the room and paid her account through Sunday, adding a healthy bonus that brought a faint smile to Rosa's dark eyes.

Belle appeared sooner than he would have thought, carrying her shoulder bag and suitcase. Evidently her nervous anticipation over seeing her mother had made her hurry, but he had a hunch she'd always been a punctual person. Another trait he couldn't help but applaud.

He took the luggage from her and ushered her out to his car. For the second time in two days he was taking her home. A great deal had changed since yesterday morning, when he'd gone to bed after being up all night with Concetta.

Leon no longer questioned why his assistant's phone call to the villa had prompted him to get dressed and go down to the bank for an explanation. It appeared there'd been a grand design at work in more ways than one. Even so, the thought raised the hairs on the back of his neck.

# CHAPTER FOUR

An hour after getting settled in the fabulous guest bedroom she'd only glimpsed yesterday, Belle heard a tap on the door. She'd been drying her freshly washed hair with her blow-dryer, and turned it off to go answer. Dinner wouldn't be for another hour.

"The *signore* sent me to find out if you need laundry service or would like something ironed for tonight," said the maid standing there.

Belle had never had service like this in her life. Since she wanted to look perfect for her mother, she decided to take advantage of Leon's incredible hospitality. But she couldn't forget for a second that his life and the lives of their parents were unique in the annals of Italian history.

"Just a moment, please."

She hurried over to her suitcase, which he'd placed on a chest at the end of the king-size bed. After opening it, she pulled out the short-sleeved, lime-colored suit with white lapels and white trim.

"This needs a little touching up to get out the wrinkles," she explained as she handed it to the maid.

"I'll be right back."

"Thank you very much."

While Belle waited, she finished brushing her naturally curly hair and put on her pearl earrings. Fastening the matching pearl necklace presented problems because she was all thumbs. Tonight would be the culmination of her dreams. Despite Leon's compliments, the fear that she'd be a disappointment to her mother wouldn't leave her alone.

She was glad she'd brought her low-slung white heels. When she'd packed for her trip, she hadn't really imagined having an opportunity to wear them.

Before long, the maid brought Belle's suit to the bedroom. "The *signore* said you should join him on the patio whenever you're ready," she announced.

Just the thought of him sent Belle's heart crashing to her feet. She could still feel his mouth on hers, filling her with an ecstasy she didn't know was possible.

Trying to pull herself together, she thanked

the maid again. One more glance in the ornate, floor-length mirror after fastening the buttons, and she felt ready to join her host. Would he approve?

What if he didn't? Did it matter to her personally?

Yes, it mattered. Horribly. Those moments of intimacy at the pension had been a revelation to her. The way he'd kissed her had brought every nerve ending to life. The fact that he was her stepbrother didn't matter once they'd crossed the line. What happened between them had shaken her so badly she could hardly function right now, but she had to!

Not wanting to keep Leon waiting, she gave one more glance to the photo she'd placed on the dresser, then left the room and started down the hall. She knew her way out to the patio, but before she reached the open French doors, a darling brown dog rushed over to greet her. As she paused to rub his head, she saw that Leon wasn't alone.

Her eyes traveled to the dainty, dark blonde baby he held in his arms. She was wearing a pink pinafore and tiny pink sandals, the colors of which stood out against the black silk shirt he was wearing. The child cuddled to his chest couldn't be more than six or seven months old and possessed features finer than bone china.

He was walking her around the patio. As he talked to her, he kissed her cheek and neck over and over again. The scene with the baby was so sweet it brought hot tears to Belle's eyes. To be loved like that...

She shivered. She knew what those lips felt like on her mouth. To her shame, she hadn't wanted him to stop. Right now she longed to feel them against her own neck.

Was the baby *his* child? Or could she be Dante's? Belle didn't know much about his family. Their coloring was so different, given Leon's vibrant black hair, but his affection for the little girl touched Belle to the core.

He must have sensed Belle's arrival. When he turned, their gazes fused. She felt him taking in her appearance. In that moment his eyes glowed a crystalline gray that made her legs go weak in response. It was that same smoldering look she'd glimpsed back at the pension after she'd pulled away from him.

"I can see you've already met Rufo. Now come and meet my daughter, Concetta."

"*Your* baby?" Belle cried in wonder. That explained the love he showered on her. "Oh," she crooned softly, "you sweet little thing."

She touched the hand clutching her daddy's shirt.

"I've seen a lot of babies in my life at the orphanage, but I never saw one who had your exquisite features and skin. You're like a porcelain doll." She looked up at Leon. "She must have gotten those dark brown eyes from her mother."

"Concetta inherited my wife's looks."

"Obviously she was a beauty."

He pressed a kiss to his daughter's forehead. "Before you judge me too harshly, I didn't mention my daughter to you before now because we had a greater issue on our minds. I planned to introduce you after you agreed to follow through and meet Luciana."

"You don't have to explain. I understand. Would you think me too presumptuous to ask how your wife died?"

"No. She passed away giving birth."

"Oh no! How awful for her—for you…" Belle's gaze traveled back to the baby. "You lost your mommy? No little girl as sweet as you should grow up without your mother. I—I'm so sorry, darling." Her voice broke. "At least you'll always know who she was, because you have your daddy, who loved her so much. And you have pictures."

Without conscious thought Belle kissed

that little hand before she looked up at Leon. "What went wrong during the delivery?"

He cuddled his daughter closer. "Soon after our marriage Benedetta was diagnosed with systemic lupus."

A moan escaped Belle's lips before she could prevent it. "One of the sisters at the orphanage had that disease."

He kissed the baby's head. "My wife was the daughter of the now deceased head of the kennel on my father's estate. She and I had been friends throughout childhood. Later on, after I came home from college and had been working at the bank for several years, we fell in love, and got married in a small, quiet ceremony, out of the public eye.

"Before long her illness became more aggressive. She developed a deep vein thrombosis in the leg, which was hidden at the time. A piece of blood clot broke off and ended up in her lung. It caused it to collapse, and heart failure followed."

"Oh, Leon…"

"Concetta came premature. My great sadness was that Benedetta's life had been snuffed out before she'd been able to hold our baby."

Belle's heart ached for them. "Will Concetta get lupus?"

"No. Thankfully, the pediatrician says my daughter is free of the disease. It doesn't necessarily follow that the child inherits it."

"Thank heaven!" Belle exclaimed. "How lucky she is to have her daddy! Every girl needs her father."

Leon's glance penetrated to the core of her being. "You think it's possible to do double duty?" he rasped.

In that question, she heard a vulnerability she would never have expected to come from him. The dark prince who'd kissed her hungrily had a weakness, after all. A precious cherub, the reminder of the woman he'd loved and lost. "With her father loving her more than anyone else in the world, she won't know anything else, and will have all the love she needs, to last her a lifetime and beyond."

He hugged his daughter tighter. "I hope you're right."

"I *know* I am. Do you think she'd get upset if I tried to hold her?"

"She isn't used to people except my staff and family. If you try, you'll be taking your life in your hands, but if you want to risk it…" He didn't sound unwilling, just skeptical.

"I do." The operation at the orphanage was

such that the older children always helped with the infants and toddlers. Belle had no hesitation as she plucked the baby from his powerful arms.

By now Concetta had started to cry, but Belle whirled around with her and sang a song that so surprised the baby, she stopped crying and looked up at her. The dog followed them. It was then Leon's little girl discovered the pearls, and grabbed them. Belle laughed gently. "You like those, don't you."

At this point Leon attempted to intervene. She felt his fingers against her skin while he tried to remove his daughter's hands, but she held on tighter. After a slight tug-of-war, the necklace broke and the pearls rolled all over the patio tiles. The sound sent Rufo chasing after them.

"Uh-oh." Belle chuckled again, because the surprise on the baby's dear face was priceless. "Where did they go?" Concetta turned her head one way, then another, trying to find them.

"I'm sorry about your necklace, Belle," Leon murmured, while his gaze narrowed on her mouth. Heat radiated through her body to her face.

"It's nothing," she said in a ragged voice.

"Once the pearls are gathered, I'll have them restrung for you."

"Don't you dare," she said, to fight her physical attraction to Concetta's father, who suddenly looked frustrated. His baby made him so human, her heart warmed to him. "This is costume jewelry I bought for twenty dollars on sale. We don't care, do we, Concetta." She kissed her head and kept walking with her, to put Leon out of her mind. Of course, it didn't work.

"Let's watch that boat with the red-and-white sail." She pointed to it, but by now the baby was staring at her. There were no more tears. "I bet you're wondering who I am. My name is Belle Donatello. I can't believe I know my last name. Your generous daddy is letting me stay here for a few days."

*I'm staying at my peril.*

She lifted her head to find Leon standing a few feet away. "How do you say *daddy* in Italian?"

"Papà," he answered in a husky tone.

Belle turned so Concetta could see him. "There's your *papà*."

All of a sudden his daughter started to whimper, and reached for him. Belle closed the distance and gave her back to him. But the baby quickly looked around and kept staring at Belle in fascination.

Leon's sharp intake of breath reached her ears. "If I hadn't witnessed it with my own eyes, I wouldn't have believed what just happened."

"What do you mean?"

"She didn't break into hysterics with you. Anything but."

Belle's mouth curved upward. "I learned in the orphanage that all babies have hysterics. It's normal. The trick is to get their attention before they become uncontrollable. The sisters were lucky, since between their habits and crucifixes, they were able to quiet the babies down fast. My pearls did rather nicely, don't you think?"

Leon had a very deep, attractive chuckle. "I think the next time you hold her, you'd better keep her hands away from the pearls in your earlobes. Inexpensive as they might be, the rest of you is…irreplaceable."

A certain nuance in his voice made her realize he'd been remembering what had gone on earlier. It wasn't something you could forget.

"Did you hear that, Concetta?" She poked the child's tummy and got a smile out of her. Lifting the hem of the pinafore, she said,

"Pink is my favorite color, too. I bet your *papà* bought this for you because he couldn't resist seeing you in it." The gleam in his eyes verified her statement. "Even if you weren't a real princess, you look like one."

For the first time since she'd joined him, his features hardened. "There are no titles under this roof and never will be."

Meaning even after his father died? It followed that, being the elder brother, he *would* be Count Malatesta one day, but he'd just made it clear he wanted no part of it.

"After what I've learned of my mother's tragic history, I think that's the wisest decision you could make as her father."

He switched Concetta to his other compact shoulder. "Before she and my father arrive, this little one needs her dinner. I'll take her to the kitchen."

"Can I come, too, and help feed her?"

A quick, white smile transformed him into the kind of man her roommates would say was jaw-dropping gorgeous. He *was* that, and so much more Belle couldn't find words. "If you do, you may have to change your outfit."

She sent him a reciprocal smile, attempting like mad to pretend she hadn't experienced rapture. "That'll be no problem."

Together with the dog, they walked through the dayroom and down another hall. Belle glimpsed a library and an elegant dining room on their way to the kitchen. From one of the windows she could see a swimming pool surrounded by ornamental flowering trees. A vision of the two of them in the water after dark wouldn't leave her alone.

In the kitchen three women were busily working. Leon introduced her to his house-keeper, Simona, the maid, Carla, and the nanny, Talia, who reached for the baby. If they knew who Belle really was, rather than simply being a guest, they showed no evidence.

After tying a bib around Concetta's neck, Talia placed her in the high chair next to the table and drew a chair over to feed her.

Belle shot Leon an imploring glance. "Could I give her her dinner?"

He looked surprised. "You really want to? Sometimes she doesn't cooperate."

"That's all right. I'd love it! I moved out of my adoptive parents' house at eighteen and haven't tended a baby since."

To her joy, he said something to Talia in Italian. She smiled at Belle, then brought the baby food jars to the table. Belle opened the lid on the meat.

"Hmm…smells like lamb." She glanced down at the dog, who sat there begging her with his eyes. "Sorry, this food isn't for you, Rufo." The other jar contained squash. "Oh boy, Concetta. This all looks nummy." Belle took the spoon and dipped it in the vegetable. "Here it comes."

Slowly, she lifted it in the air and did a few maneuvers. Those black-brown eyes followed the action faithfully. Belle brought the spoon closer to the baby, who'd already opened her mouth, waiting for her food. Belle saw Leon in the shape of his daughter's mouth and felt an adrenaline rush that almost caused her to drop the utensil.

He burst into laughter. "You're a natural mother."

"Not really." She began feeding Concetta her meat while the women watched. "I fed the babies at the orphanage. This is the only thing I have a natural aptitude for."

"The CEO at TCCPI has told me otherwise," he stated.

If she wasn't careful, she might start wanting to hear more of his compliments. *And believing them, Belle?*

"When you're on your own and forced to earn a living, you learn a trade fast."

A troubled expression entered his eyes.

"Your adoptive father never helped you after you left home?"

She shook her head, with its dark, shiny mass of flowing hair, and continued to feed the baby. "But I'd be ungrateful if I didn't acknowledge that he and Nadine fed and clothed me for eight years while I lived under their roof. Some of my friends in the orphanage never got adopted, and lived their whole lives there until they were old enough to leave. I was one of the luckier ones."

Concetta hadn't quite finished her food when she put her hands out as if to say she was full. She was so adorable, Belle could hardly stand it. "I think you've had enough." Without thinking about it, she untied the bib. After wiping Concetta's mouth with it, she put it on the table and lifted the baby out of the high chair.

"Uh-oh. I can tell you need to be changed. Where's your bedroom?"

Leon had been lounging against the wall, watching them. "Upstairs."

Belle darted him a glance. "If you'll show me, I'll change her, but only if it's all right with you."

One black brow lifted. "Since you've got her literally eating out of the palm of your hand, I have a feeling she'd have a meltdown if anyone else dared to interfere at this point."

"Leon…" The man had lethal charm. It had been getting to her from the first day and had worked its way beneath her skin.

"Follow me."

The only thing to do was concentrate on the baby. "You have the most beautiful home, Concetta. I always wanted to live in a house with a staircase like this. I wonder how long it will be before you slide down the banister when your *papà* isn't looking."

She heard the low chuckles trailing after him, and it was impossible to keep her eyes off his hard-muscled frame. She knew what it was like to be crushed against him, and came close to losing her breath, remembering. In father mode, Leon was completely different from the forbidding male she'd first met. Like this he was irresistible.

Rufo darted ahead of them. They entered the first room at the top of the stairs. "I might have known you'd live in a nursery like this. Your father has spoiled you silly, you lucky little girl." Belle felt as if she'd entered fairyland. He'd supplied everything a child could ever want.

There was a photograph on the dresser of a lovely, dark blonde woman who had to be

Leon's deceased wife. Concetta would always ache for the mother who hadn't lived through childbirth. The thought made Belle's heart constrict. She knew what it felt like to want your mother and never know her.

She carried the baby over to the changing table against the wall and got busy. After powdering, she put a clean diaper on her. Concetta's cooperation made it an easy operation.

Leon stood next to Belle. The scent of the soap he used in the shower lingered to torment her.

"You've mesmerized my daughter."

"It's the lime suit." She picked up the baby. After giving her a kiss on her neck, she placed Concetta in her father's arms. "I'm wearing a different color than she's used to seeing."

"So that's your secret weapon?"

When Belle raised her head in query, the crystal gray eyes she remembered had morphed to a slate color. Just now she'd detected an edge in his tone, and didn't understand it. If he hadn't wanted her to feed or change the baby, he should have told her.

As her spirits plummeted, she heard a male voice, and spun around to discover Leon's father in the nursery doorway. Rufo had already hurried over to him. She recognized him from the photographs, but since the time those pictures were taken, his dark hair had become streaked with silver.

His presence meant Belle's mother was here! Her mouth went dry.

Leon saw the shock on his father's face. Normally, he headed straight for Concetta, but not this time. The count was staring at Belle. Her beauty stopped men in their tracks, but he'd also seen the resemblance to Luciana and was obviously speechless for a moment.

His father wasn't the only one. Leon had felt out of control since their first meeting. Just now her easy interaction with Concetta, and his daughter's acceptance of Belle, had caught him unaware. It had to be because Belle reminded her of Luciana. To his chagrin he'd experienced a ridiculous moment of jealousy.

"Papà? May I introduce Belle Peterson. Belle? Meet my father, Sullisto."

The older man walked over to Belle with suspiciously bright eyes. "It's like seeing your beautiful mother when she was in her twenties." He kissed her on both cheeks and grasped her hands. "My wife's not going to believe it. I'm not sure I do."

"I don't believe it, either," Belle answered in an unsteady voice. "It's like a dream. I'm so happy to meet you."

He studied her features for a long moment. "How do you want to do this, my dear?"

Leon appreciated his father's sensitivity and stepped in. "Where's Luciana?"

"I left her in the living room, playing the piano."

"Why don't you entertain Concetta up here while I take Belle downstairs to meet her?" He kissed the baby and handed her over. "I'll come back for the two of you in a few minutes and we'll go down together."

His father hugged the baby to him before looking at Belle. "Take all the time you need."

"Are you sure this is the right thing to do, *signore*?" Her question went straight to Leon's gut.

"Call me Sullisto. You're going to make a new person of my wife," his father reassured her.

A hand went to her throat. "Thank you for being so kind and accepting."

Leon could only wonder at the emotions gripping her. "Let's go."

She followed him out of the room and down the stairs. The sound of the piano grew louder. When they reached the front foyer, he turned to her. "Ready?"

Belle nodded. "I've been waiting for this all my life, but I'd like you to go first."

Taking a deep breath, he opened the French doors. "Good evening, Luciana."

The playing stopped and she got up from the baby grand piano looking lovely as usual in a draped midriff jersey dress in a blue print. Though her daughter wasn't wearing Versace, Belle had the same sense of style and good taste as her mother.

She hurried across the Oriental rug toward him. "Thank you for inviting us, Leon. Where's your precious baby?"

He noticed the two women had the same little tremor in their voices when they were nervous. They were both the same height, but Luciana wore her hair short these days in a stylish cut. After giving her a kiss on both cheeks, he said, "Upstairs with Papà. But before he brings her down, there's someone I want you to meet."

"A special woman?"

He knew what she was thinking. His father had Leon's love life on his mind and no doubt had been discussing the list of eligible titled women with Luciana. "This one is very special. You'll have to speak English. Come in," he called over his shoulder.

After Belle stepped into the living room, he watched Luciana's expression turn to incredulity, then shock. She went so pale he put an arm around her shoulders and helped her to the nearest love seat. "Your daughter has come all the way from New York looking for you."

A stillness enveloped both women before Luciana cried, *"Arabella?"*

Tears splashed down Belle's cheeks. She, too, had lost color. Fear that she might faint prompted Leon to help her sit next to her mother.

"That's my real name?" she asked in wonder. "Arabella?"

"Yes. Arabella Donatello Sloan. Your father was English. Arabella was his grandmother's name. She told him it meant beautiful lion. You *are* so beautiful. I don't know how you ever found me, but oh, my darling baby girl, I've missed and ached for you every moment since I gave you up. You've been in my every prayer. Let me hold you."

It was like a light had gone on inside, bringing Luciana to life, illuminating her countenance. Like her mother, Belle glowed with a new radiance. They weren't aware of anyone else.

The sight of the two women clinging desperately while they communicated and wept and made dozens of comparisons brought a giant-size boulder to Leon's throat.

The explanation of Belle's name reminded Leon of his conversation with her the day before, about his own name meaning lion. Belle remembered, too, because she darted him a quick glance. It was an odd coincidence.

"I want you to know about your father. I have pictures of him back at the palazzo."

Belle flashed Leon a smile. He knew what seeing a picture of him would do for her.

"Arabella was the grandmother who raised him before she died. We talked about names before you were born. That's the one we liked the best. You would have loved him, but he was killed before we could be married. I was so terrified he'd been murdered that, when I had you, I made the decision to give you up because the danger you might be killed, too, was too great."

Leon moved closer to them. "We now know that no one was murdered, and Robert's death had to have been an accident."

"Yes, but I didn't know it until a few

months ago. When I think about the years we've lost…" Her mother broke down sobbing.

Belle held her for a long time. "What happened to my father?"

"Robert and I had been in downtown Newburgh and we'd just left each other. He'd started across the intersection when this car crossed over the lines and came at him at full speed. The driver just kept going, leaving Robert lying there lifeless."

Belle's groan filled the room.

"It was so horrifying I went into labor and was taken to the hospital. You came a month early, Arabella. You were still in the intensive care unit when I had a graveside service for Robert. The police never found the man who killed him."

"How terrible for you." Belle reached out to hug her harder.

"It *was* terrible, since I couldn't tell my father. He didn't know about Robert. I knew if I took you back to Italy, he wouldn't let me keep you at the palazzo. Worse, I was afraid you wouldn't be safe with me anywhere.

"When I made arrangements for you at the orphanage, you still needed a lot of care. But my father sent for me to come home. He wasn't feeling well, because of his heart, and hinted that he wanted me to meet Count Malatesta, who'd recently lost his wife to cancer. My father wanted him for a son-in-law.

"We married on my twentieth birthday. The fact that he still wanted me after I confessed everything to him in private proved to me he was a good man. But while I was still in New York, I couldn't imagine ever marrying again. It was agony, because I had to rely on the sisters to watch over you. I told them I'd named you Belle. That way no one could ever trace you to Robert or me. I also told them they had to promise that whoever adopted you would take you to church."

"Nadine always took me."

"Thank heaven for that."

In all the years Leon had known Luciana, she'd never made such long speeches. In one breath he'd already learned enough about her past to erase the lies he'd heard whispered by the staff and others who lived on gossip. Those lies about her being shallow and of little substance had colored his thinking for years.

He left the living room and remained outside the doors for several minutes to get a grip on his emotions, before taking the stairs two at a time. When he entered the nursery, he found his father helping Concetta stack some blocks. Sullisto saw him in the doorway. "Well…I guess I don't have to ask how it went. Your eyes say it all."

Leon nodded. "You were right. This was one reunion that was meant to be. Come downstairs and see for yourself."

He plucked his daughter from the floor, still clutching one of her blocks, and they headed out the door with Rufo. When they'd descended the staircase and entered the living room, he discovered the two women still seated on the love seat, deep in conversation punctuated with laughter and tears.

"Forgive us for barging in on you, but my daughter wants to join in."

"Concetta…" Luciana rushed over to take her from Leon's arms. Belle was right there with her. Both women fussed over his daughter, laughing, and his little girl broke out in smile after smile. She'd never had so much loving attention in her life.

Leon glanced at his father. They shared a silent message that left no doubt this watershed moment had changed the fabric of life in both Malatesta households.

"Dinner's ready. Let's go in the dining room. Tonight we'll all eat together." Leon's words delighted the women.

After he brought the high chair in, they

both begged him to put Concetta between them at the candlelit table. Happiness reigned for the next hour, with most of the attention focused on the baby.

Leon looked around, realizing he hadn't felt this sense of family since before his own mother had died. His father hadn't seemed this relaxed and happy in years, either. As for Luciana, being united with her daughter had transformed her to the point Leon hardly recognized her. Gone were the shadows and that underlying look of depression.

But it was the new addition to his table that filled him with emotions foreign to him. Since Benedetta's death, Concetta had been the only joy in his life. Having lost his wife, he hadn't been able to think about another woman. As for marriage, he had no plan to marry again. His daughter was all he could handle, all he *wanted* to handle.

Before Benedetta had died, she'd been Leon's comfort. With two losses in his life, plus Dante's aloofness, it was Concetta who was the beat of his heart now. Though she was loved by his staff, he guarded her possessively, afraid for anything to happen to her.

He'd been functioning on automatic pilot at work, unenthusiastic about the pleasures he'd once enjoyed. His good friend Vito had phoned, no doubt to make some vacation plans, but Leon hadn't even called him back yet.

While he'd been going along in this whitewashed state, Belle Peterson had exploded onto the scene. Her presence reminded him of someone who'd come along his private stretch of beach and purposely destroyed the sand castle he'd made for his daughter with painstaking care.

In Belle's case it wasn't intentional. Far from it. But the damage was just as bad, because nothing could be put back the way it was before. Leon didn't like having his world turned upside down, leaving him with inexplicable feelings percolating to life inside.

He should never have kissed her. Obviously, he needed to start dating other women. There were many he could choose from if he wanted to. But it was disconcerting to realize that none of them measured up in any way to Belle.

When Carla came into the dining room to pour more coffee, he asked her to tell Talia to come and put the baby to bed. Concetta was too loud and squirmy, a telltale sign she was tired. But after the nanny arrived and pulled her out of her high chair, his daughter cried and fought not to be taken away. To his astonishment, she reached for Belle and quieted down the second his houseguest grasped the baby to her.

*Diavolo!* He couldn't blame it on the green suit *or* the shape in it. Belle herself, with her creative ways of doing things, had captured his daughter's interest.

Those dark blue eyes sought his with a trace of concern. "If it's all right with you, I'd love to get her ready for bed."

This wasn't supposed to happen, but what could Leon say? "I'm sure that will make Concetta very happy." When he saw the way she interacted with Belle, it came to him that his daughter needed a mother. Until now he'd been thinking only of his own needs. It had taken Belle's advent in their lives for him to realize a father wasn't enough for Concetta, who deserved two parents to make her life complete.

"Oh good! Come with me," she said to Luciana. "We'll do it together."

"You'll find a stretchy suit in the top drawer of the dresser," Leon suggested.

"A stretchy suit?" Belle said to the baby. "I wonder how many pink ones you have."

"It's a beautiful color on her, but then she's lovely in every color," Luciana said as they left the dining room, chatting together like a mother and daughter who'd never been apart. "She's already a great beauty."

Once they were alone, Sullisto eyed Leon. "I can see that Luciana won't want to be separated from Belle now that they've found each other. You say she's flying back to New York on Sunday?"

"That was the plan," Leon muttered, not able to think that far ahead.

"Well, as long as she's in Rimini, she'll stay with us at the palazzo. I'm anxious to get them both home." After a slight hesitation, he said, "I haven't told Luciana this yet, but I'm planning to adopt Belle so she'll be an integral part of the family."

After learning how much Luciana had suffered since giving up her daughter, Leon wasn't surprised by the announcement. What it did do was convince him how deeply his father had learned to love Belle's mother.

Feeling restless with troubling thoughts he hadn't sorted out yet, Leon got to his feet. "I'll go up and make sure Concetta is settling down without problem. Have you told Dante about Belle?"

"No. Pia has been so upset because she hasn't conceived yet, he took her to Florence for a little break. They won't be back until sometime tomorrow afternoon. It's probably a good thing. I want to give Luciana and Belle the next twelve hours or so together before we break the news to them.

"They don't have your advantage of getting to know Belle first, and her reasons for coming to Rimini. It will take time for him and Pia to absorb everything that's happened while they've been gone."

Dante wouldn't be the only one. Leon was still attempting to deal with the reality of Luciana's daughter, whose response had almost sent him into cardiac arrest earlier. Sullisto had been brilliant at keeping his wife's secret from their family. But for some reason his plan to adopt Belle didn't sit well with Leon.

He left his father at the table and went to the kitchen to find Talia, asking her to get Concetta's bottle ready and take it upstairs. "You outdid yourself on the dinner," he said to Simona, before bounding up the staircase.

He found a beaming Luciana holding his daughter, who'd been changed into a white stretchy suit with feet. Belle stood next to them, playing with his daughter's toes. The baby was laughing out loud.

Luciana saw him first. "Oh, Leon, she's the dearest child in the whole world." There was a new light in her eyes.

Belle's expression reflected the same sentiment. "We wish she didn't have to go to bed."

"I'm sure she doesn't want to be put down, either, but it's time." He walked over and reached for his daughter, who clung to him with satisfying eagerness. Talia wasn't far behind with the bottle.

She sat down in the rocker, so he could hand her the baby, who'd started to fuss the second he let go of her. "*Buonanotte,* Concetta. Be a good girl for Talia." He kissed her cheeks before following the two women out of the nursery.

Sullisto met them at the bottom of the stairs. He reached for Belle's hand. "Your mother and I would like you to stay at the palazzo with us while you're in Rimini. Would you like to come with us now?"

Leon sensed her slight hesitation. He was pleased by it when he shouldn't have been. Though he didn't know what was going on in her mind, he made the instant decision to intervene.

"Belle has already settled in as my houseguest for tonight, Papà. As it's late and I know she's exhausted, why don't I bring her to the palazzo in the morning for breakfast, and we'll discuss future plans?"

Luciana hugged her daughter. "Of course you're tired. After the shock of coming face-to-face with my beautiful daughter, whom I thought would always be lost to me, I confess I am, too. Tomorrow we'll spend the whole day together. I can't wait."

"Neither can I."

"I love you, Arabella."

"I love you, too." Belle's words came out in a whisper.

They hugged for a long time before letting each other go. Together everyone moved to the front foyer. Luciana's gaze moved to Leon. "Please bring Concetta when you come. We can't get enough of her."

Leon nodded to his stepmother and father before the two of them disappeared out the door. When it closed he turned to Belle.

"Did I speak too soon for you? It's not too late to go with them."

She shook her head. "Actually, I'm very grateful you said what you did. No matter what you say, this meeting put my mother and your father in a difficult position. By my staying here in your home, they'll have time to talk alone tonight. She put on a wonderful front, but—"

"It was no front," Leon contradicted. "I've known her close to fourteen years. The joy on her face when she saw you changed her to the point that I hardly recognized her."

Belle bit her lip. "But that doesn't alter the fact that she gave me up and no one knew about it. Now that I'm here, she has to worry about people finding out she had a child before she married your father."

"Do you honestly believe that matters to either of them now?"

"I don't know. She said she gave me up to keep me safe. But since that's no longer a concern and I've shown up, she'll have to deal with gossip. I'm not worried for myself, but the last thing I want is to bring more unhappiness to your family."

"That's very noble of you, Belle, but she's already let you know you're welcome with open arms."

Her chin lifted. "Maybe. I think it would be better if she comes over here in the morning, where we can talk in private before I go back to New York. Her presence in your home won't draw attention. If I thought my coming to Italy could upset her life in any way…"

He raked a hand through his hair. "Come out on the patio with me and we'll talk."

Without saying anything, she followed him down the hall to the other part of the house.

When he opened the doors to the patio, they were greeted by a sea breeze scented with the fragrance of the garden flowers. Belle walked over to the railing. "How absolutely heavenly it is out here."

"It's my favorite place."

"I can see why."

Leon stood next to her, studying her stunning profile, which was half hidden by her dark hair. "Forget everything else for a minute and answer me one question."

She turned her head in his direction. "You want to know how I feel."

Belle had the disarming habit of being able to read his mind. "Can you put it into words yet?"

"No," she answered promptly. "Luciana is wonderful. More wonderful than I could have ever hoped. So's your father. But over these years, this need to find her has been all about me and what I want. Sitting with her on the love seat while she explained her life to me, I realized what a terrible thing I've done to her."

Leon looked into those blue eyes glittering with tears. "I don't understand."

"She didn't deserve to have me sweep into her world, bringing up all the pain and unhappiness she's put behind her. No—" Belle put up her hands when he would have argued with her.

"The sister in charge warned me I could be taking a great risk in trying to find my birth mother. I thought I knew better when you told me I could meet her at dinner tonight. When I met your father, I still felt good about it. But I don't anymore."

Leon had to think fast. "I'm guessing the part of you that feels unlovable has taken over for the moment. You're terrified that any more time spent with her and she'll see all your flaws."

Belle gripped the railing tighter. "I'm nothing like her. She's lovely and refined. I never met anyone so gracious. She's not the kind of person to tell you what she's really thinking inside. She and your father have made a life together. There's no place in it for me and there shouldn't have to be."

"You're wrong about that, Belle." If his father had his way, it wouldn't be long before she found herself being adopted for the second time in her life.

"It's hard to explain, but I feel like I've trespassed on their lives."

"Trespassed… If you feel like that, then blame me for facilitating the meeting."

Tears again sparkled in her eyes. "I could

have decided not to go through with the plans for this evening. Of course I don't blame you. You've been wonderful. You *all* have. I'm the one who doesn't belong in Rimini."

"That's another part of you talking, the part that feels you don't deserve this outpouring of kindness and acceptance. You're going to have to give this time, Belle. In the past you've been too used to rejection from your adoptive father and brother. If you turn away now, after one meeting, you'll be giving in to old habits. Consider your mother's feelings."

"She's all I'm thinking about right now."

"How do you imagine she'll feel if you let your fear of rejection prevent her from really getting to know you? It works both ways."

Belle shook her head. "I don't know what to do."

"Do you think *she* does?"

A troubled sigh escaped her lips. "I'm not sure. If she'd begged me to come with her tonight..."

Ah. "What if she was afraid to pressure you, in case you had reservations? I'm the one who mentioned your fatigue, and she grabbed on to it for an excuse, in case you didn't feel comfortable going with them. Don't you see?"

"I—I don't know what I see," Belle stammered. "I love her so much already, Leon, but I'm more anxious than ever." Her eyes met his, full of despair and confusion.

He wasn't immune to her pain, but he couldn't take her in his arms again, not after he'd sworn to keep his distance.

Yesterday, when he'd drawn her against him, he'd become instantly aware of her as an alluring woman, but he'd fought those feelings. He couldn't handle the complication of a woman in his life. Yet when they'd been at the pension, he'd reached for her again, because he couldn't help himself. Much more of this and he would lose every bit of objectivity.

Already her presence was making chaos of the well-ordered existence he'd been putting back together since Benedetta's death. Otherwise why would he have stepped in to suggest Belle remain under his roof tonight?

# CHAPTER FIVE

BELLE LOOKED AWAY from Leon's dark gaze, trying desperately to pull herself together. After priding herself on being able to handle her life on her own, why did she keep falling apart like this?

She should have jumped at the opportunity to go home with her mother earlier, but Leon had read her hesitation with uncanny accuracy and had offered another solution. When she'd confided her reason to him for holding back, she'd told the truth. She'd wanted to give her mother space.

But she feared there'd been another reason to stay with Leon, not so readily discernible until this moment, now that she was alone with him again. Reflecting back to that interlude in her bedroom at the pension, she was angered by her need for comfort from the last person she should have turned to.

For her to have lost control and kissed a

man who still had to be grieving the loss of his wife was humiliating. It was madness.

Feigning a calm she didn't feel, she managed to dredge up a smile. "Thank you for helping me work through my angst. Concetta is the luckiest little girl in the world to have you for her father. And like *your* father, you're a virtual bulwark of strength and reason, Leon Malatesta. I've gotten over my jitters and can go to bed now with the hope of getting some sleep. Good night."

Without looking at him, she left the patio and went straight to the guest bedroom, shutting the door.

A good sleep? That was hilarious.

*"Signorina?"*

Belle came out of the bathroom the next morning, where she'd been putting on her makeup. Earlier, Carla had brought her coffee. "Yes, Simona?"

"Signor Malatesta says to come to the rear foyer. He's ready to drive you to the palazzo whenever you're ready."

"I'll be right there. Thank you."

She'd been up for an hour, unable to stay in bed following a restless night's sleep. After some experimenting, she drew her hair back at the nape. In her ears she'd put on her favorite pink topaz earrings. Luciana was so elegant, Belle wanted to look her best for her mother.

This morning she'd dressed in a short-sleeved, three-piece suit of dusky pink, with a paler pink shell. Whenever she wore it to the regional meetings for her work, it garnered compliments.

When she stepped outside the door, she saw Leon in a light tan suit, fastening his daughter in the back car seat of a dark blue luxury sedan. Concetta was dressed in a blue-and-yellow sunsuit. With those dark brown eyes that saw Belle coming, she was a picture.

"Good morning, you adorable thing!"

He stood up, transferring his gaze to Belle. "*Buon giorno,* Arabella," he murmured, while his eyes traveled over every inch of her. When he did that, she melted on the spot.

"*Buon giorno,*" she responded, sounding too American for words. "Do you mind if I sit in back with her?" During the night Belle had decided that the only safe way to be around Leon was to stay close to his daughter. It was no penance. Belle was already crazy about her.

Without waiting for an answer, she walked

around to the other side and climbed in back. Rufo had already made his place on the floor at the baby's feet. Belle rubbed his head behind his ears. He licked her hand before she turned to Concetta and fastened her own seat belt.

"How's my little sweetie? I love those cute seashells on your top." As she touched them, the baby smiled and reached out to pull her hair.

Leon was still looking in from the other side. Could there be such a striking man anywhere else in existence? "Like I said last night, you keep that up at your own risk."

"After the pearls, what's a little hair?" she teased.

He chuckled. "She's already got her sights set on your earrings. They're stunning on you, by the way."

"Thank you." *Please don't keep saying personal things like that to me.*

In seconds he got behind the wheel and drove them away from the estate toward the city. This was the first time since coming to Rimini that Belle was actually able to see it through a tourist's eyes. Until now her thoughts had been so focused on finding her mother, she'd been pretty much unobservant.

He drove her along the autostrada and

played tour guide. On one side were hundreds of fabulous-looking hotels. On the other were hundreds and hundreds of colorful umbrellas set up three rows deep on the famous twelve-mile-long stretch of beach.

"It's a sun lover's paradise, Leon!"

"If you don't mind the invasion of masses of humanity," he drawled over his shoulder.

But he didn't have to worry about that. His private portion of beach was off-limits, and no doubt strictly watched by his security men.

After a few minutes they climbed a slight elevation where an incredible period residence in an orangey-pink color came into view. "Oh, Leon…"

"This is the Malatesta palazzo. Our family purchased it in the nineteenth century. It's of moderate size, but over the years has been restored and transformed. Like many of the elegant patrician villas along this section of the Adriatic, it combines modern technology with old-world charm." He drove through the gates, past cypress trees and a fantastic maze.

"It's breathtaking. When you were little, your friends must have thought they'd died and gone to heaven when you invited them over to play."

His eyes gleamed with amusement as he looked at her through the rearview mirror. "I don't know about that, but Dante and I enjoyed hiding out from the staff. Guests have been known to get lost in there."

"I don't doubt it."

They continued on and wound around the fountain to the front entrance. Thrilled to see her mother come out the door and rush over to her side of the car, Belle hurriedly got out to meet her. They hugged for a long time.

"Now I know last night wasn't a dream." Luciana cupped her face. "My dearest girl, do you think you could ever bring yourself to call me Mom? You don't have to, but—"

"I wanted to call you Mom last night," Belle confessed.

"Then it's settled. Come on. Let's get Concetta and go inside." Belle looked around, to discover Leon had his daughter in his arms. "We're eating on the terrace," her mother announced. "I've got Concetta's high chair set up."

Rufo ran ahead to where Sullisto stood in the elegant foyer. He sought out Belle with such a warm smile that she had to believe it was a sincere reflection of how he felt about her. It went a long way to dispel some of her fears for her intrusion in their lives.

She felt Leon's gaze. When she looked up, his gray eyes seemed to encourage her to embrace what was happening.

Once she was inside, the palazzo's sumptuous tapestries and marble floors left her speechless. Belle particularly loved the colonnade with its stained-glass windows. Leon explained that before the destruction in the war, they'd formed part of the chapel.

After following the passageway, they came out to the terrace, where a veritable feast awaited them. But Belle couldn't hold back her cry of wonder at the sunken garden below. Grass surrounded a giant black-and-white chessboard. Statues of Roman gods were placed in the odd squares, each depicting one of the twelve months of the year.

"I've never seen anything like it! The whole estate is unreal." Her gaze unconsciously flew to Leon's. "To think this was your playground, growing up."

His eyes smiled back at her.

"Come and sit by me, darling. Here are some pictures of your father."

Belle did her mother's bidding. Her hands shook as she studied the half-dozen snapshots. "He looks so young and handsome!" She couldn't believe she was gazing at her own father.

"He was both. Keep those photos. I have more."

After studying them, Belle put them carefully in her purse. Over the delicious meal, she lost track of time, answering her mother's questions about life at the orphanage. Then the subject turned to the Petersons.

Sullisto shook his head. "I can't understand why you weren't adopted right off as a baby."

"I used to ask the sisters the same thing. They told me that because I was premature, I was very sickly. It seems I took a long time to get well, and was underdeveloped. My speech didn't come until I was about four. By then, I was too old."

"Darling…" Luciana hugged her for a long time before she let Belle go.

"It's all right. I finally did get adopted, but I didn't see love between Nadine and Ben. I guess somewhere deep down he cared for her, enough to go along with my adoption. But I wished I'd been placed in a foster home, so I could have left when things got difficult."

"You had no advocate?" her mom asked, sounding horrified.

"Not after being adopted. But at one point I gathered enough courage to talk to her about it. She said she'd wanted me to feel like I belonged. Nadine had the right instincts, but there was too much wrong in their marriage, and I know for a fact they didn't consult Cliff. He was so angry, I got out of the house the second I turned eighteen. As you know, they were killed in a car crash later on."

Her mother's eyes had filled with sadness. "Where did you go, darling?"

"I'd been scanning the classifieds and found a want ad for a roommate. I went to meet three single girls who'd rented part of an old house and could fit one more person. I told them that if they'd give me a month, I'd get a job and move in. Since I needed a cell phone, I applied for work at TCCPI and they hired me. That was my lucky day."

"Now she's a manager," Leon interjected. He'd just gotten up from the table to walk Concetta around. "In fact, the corporation is taking her in to the head office in New York City in two months."

Belle's head flew back. "You didn't tell me that earlier. You only said I was going to be promoted."

His features sobered. "I overstepped my boundaries when I contacted them, and didn't want to give away all the surprises in store for you."

He'd surprised her again.

"That's wonderful!" Luciana exclaimed, but a look of pain had crossed over her face, belying her words. "Do you love your work?"

Bemused by the question, Belle turned to her mother. She knew what she was really asking. They'd met only last evening. After finding her parent, the idea of separation was unthinkable to her right now, too. "I like it well enough. It's been a way to earn a living, and they've been paying for me to go to college at night. Another semester and I'll get my business degree."

"I'm so proud of you! Are you still living with roommates?"

"Yes. It's cheaper and I've been able to save some money." Belle pulled the wallet out of her handbag and passed around some pictures of her friends. She had one photo of the Peterson family to show them.

After studying the photos, Sullisto leaned forward. "I must admit I'm surprised you didn't show us the picture of your latest love interest. Why aren't you married? Are the men in America blind? Who's the miserable man you're driving crazy at the moment?"

Belle laughed quietly. "I've been too busy

with studies, along with trying to put my store on top, to get into a relationship."

"You sound like Leonardo," he grumbled.

"Concetta keeps me so occupied, there's no room for anyone else."

She sensed a certain friction between him and his father. Belle happened to know how deeply enamored Leon was of his little girl. It surprised her Sullisto would touch on that subject, when he had to know his son was still grieving over his wife's death. No wonder she'd detected an underlying trace of impatience in Leon's response.

Belle could only envy the woman who would one day come into his life and steal his heart. As she struggled with the possibility that he might always love Benedetta too much to move on, she heard footsteps in the background, and turned her head to see an attractive man and woman dressed in expensive-looking sport clothes walk out on the terrace.

"Ah, Dante!" Sullisto got to his feet to embrace his son, who bore a superficial likeness to him and Leon. "We didn't expect you until this afternoon," he said in English. "You've arrived back from Florence just in time to meet our home's most honored guest. Belle

Peterson from New York? This is my son Dante, and his lovely wife, Pia."

Belle agreed Pia was charming, with amber eyes and strawberry-blond hair she wore in a stylish bob. They walked around and shook her hand before taking their places at the table. But already Belle felt uncomfortable, because Leon's brother had seen her sitting next to Luciana, and had to have noticed the resemblance. He kept staring at them. So did his wife, who whispered something to him.

Sullisto turned to his wife. "*Cara?* Why don't you carry on from here?"

Luciana cleared her throat and got to her feet. Belle's gaze collided with Leon's oddly speculative glance. She had the impression he didn't know how this was going to play out, and she felt an odd chill go through her.

"After all these years, my greatest dream has come true." She reached for Belle's hand and clung to it. "Years ago my father sent me to New York, because he thought I was in danger here.

"You know the family history, but there are some things no one ever knew except your father, who loved me enough to marry me anyway. You'll never know what that love did for me and how much I've grown to love him since then."

Her mother's revelations brought moisture to Sullisto's eyes and touched Belle to the depths of her soul. But as she saw a bewildered look creep over Dante's face, the blood started to throb at her temples.

"While I was there, I met a man from England named Robert Sloan, and we fell in love. When we found out we were expecting a baby, we planned to be married with or without my father's permission. But Robert was killed in a hit-and-run accident. At the time I was convinced he'd been murdered, and it brought on early labor for me."

Dante looked like a victim of shell shock. As Luciana continued talking, he transferred his cold gaze to Belle. It reminded her of Cliff's menacing eyes when his mother had first introduced them. That memory made her shrink inside as Luciana came to the end of the story.

"Her real name is Arabella Donatello Sloan. She flew to Rimini this week to try and find me. If it weren't for Leon, we would never have been reunited."

Dante turned to his brother. A stream of unintelligible Italian poured from his mouth.

"Our guest doesn't speak Italian," Leon

reminded him. For an instant his gray eyes trapped Belle's as reams of unspoken thoughts passed between them. This was the crisis Belle had prayed wouldn't happen.

Sullisto intervened and in English told Dante how she'd researched the Donatello name until it came to Leon's attention at the bank.

"It's an absolute miracle," Luciana interjected. "It's one that has brought me the greatest happiness you can imagine. Sullisto and I talked it over last night. We're hoping she'll decide to make her home here at the palazzo with all of us, permanently."

*"Mom..."*

While Belle was still trying to absorb the wonder of it, Sullisto tapped his crystal goblet with a fork. After clearing his throat, he said, "We want to take care of you from here on out. Now that you're united with your mother, we don't want anything to keep you two apart." He reached for Luciana's hand. "I'm planning to adopt you, Arabella."

*"Adopt?"* Belle gasped. "I—I hardly know what to say—" Her voice caught.

A smile broke out on his lips. "You don't have to say anything."

Belle was so overcome with emotions sweeping through her, she hardly noticed that Dante had gotten to his feet. With one glance, she saw that he'd lost color. He stared around the table at all of them. The dangerous glint coming from those dark depths frightened her.

"That's quite a story. The resemblance between mother and daughter is extraordinary, thus dispensing with a DNA test," he rapped out. His gaze finally fastened on Belle. "Welcome to the Malatesta family, Arabella. We truly do live up to our name, don't we?"

*"Basta!"* his father exclaimed. Belle knew what it meant.

*"Mi dispiace,* Papà," he answered with sarcasm. "Now if you'll excuse us, Pia and I have other things to do." He strode off the patio with an unhappy wife in pursuit.

"Don't look alarmed," Sullisto advised Belle the minute they were gone. "Your mother and I discussed it last night. There's no right way to handle a situation like this. We didn't expect them home until later, but since he walked in on us, we felt it was better to let Dante know up front. When he and Pia have talked about it, he'll apologize for his bad behavior."

Belle got up from the table. "For you to welcome me into your home leaves me thrilled and speechless, but I'm afraid the shock of hearing your plan to adopt me was too great for Dante. I'm not so much alarmed as sad, Sullisto. It's because my adoptive brother, Cliff, had the exact same reaction when Nadine brought me to their house from the orphanage. He was unprepared for it."

"But it's not quite the same thing," Sullisto impressed upon her. "You're flesh of Luciana's flesh. Dante is flesh of mine. Both of you are beloved to me and your mother." His words touched her to the core. "The difference lies in the fact that Dante's not a teenage boy. He's a grown man who's married, with expectations of raising a family of his own. Your being brought into the family has no bearing on his life except to enrich it."

"E-even so—" her voice faltered "—he has lived under your roof all his life and has sustained a huge shock that will impact your family and create gossip. If it's all right with you, I would feel much better if the two of you had the rest of the day to be alone with him and his wife. They're going to need to talk about this."

With an anxious glance at Leon, Belle implored him with her eyes to help her out of this, and prayed he got the message. "Since Concetta is ready for a nap, I'll go back to the villa with Leon." She leaned over to kiss her mother, then Sullisto. "Thank you for this wonderful morning. I don't deserve the gift of love you've showered on me. You have no idea how much I love both of you. Call me later."

Leon had already lifted the baby from the high chair and was ready to go. They left the palazzo and she climbed in the back of the sedan to help him fasten Concetta in the car seat. Rufo hopped in and lay down.

Belle kissed the baby's nose. "You were such a good girl this morning, you deserve a treat." She reached in her bag and pulled out her lipstick. The baby grabbed the tube and immediately put it in her mouth. It kept her occupied during the drive.

If Belle hadn't made the suggestion to escape, Leon would have insisted they leave the palazzo immediately. The shattered look on Dante's face had revealed what Leon had always suspected.

Like a volcano slowly building magma, his quiet, subdued brother had hidden his feelings beneath a facade. But today they had erupted into the stratosphere, exposing remembered pain and fresh new hurt.

"When we get back to the villa, I'll ask

Talia to put the baby to bed so you and I can talk about what's happened."

"I can't bear that I've brought all this on. It's disrupting your life and everyone else's. I didn't want to hurt Mother's feelings by leaving so fast, but when I saw poor Dante's eyes…" Belle buried her face in her hands.

"You can be sure she and Papà understood. Dante finally reacted to years of suppressed pain. His behavior wasn't directed at you. It's been coming on since the day our father told us he was getting married again."

"I feel so sorry for him."

So did Leon. He eyed her through the rearview mirror. "Do you have a swimming costume?"

She blinked. "Yes."

"Good. When you've changed back at the house, meet me on the patio and we'll go down to the beach. We both need to channel our negative energy into something physical."

Belle nodded. "You're reading my mind again. A swim is exactly what I crave."

"In that case, you'll want a beach towel. There are half a dozen on the closet shelf in the guest bathroom."

"Thank you."

The drive didn't take long. When they entered the villa he showered his loving daughter with kisses before turning her over to Talia. Once upstairs in his room he changed into his black swimming trunks.

His last task was to phone Berto and tell him he wouldn't be coming in to work. Unless there was an emergency, Leon was taking time off until tomorrow. On his way out the door he grabbed a towel.

It didn't surprise him to find Belle in bare feet, waiting for him on the patio. The woman needed to talk. He could sense her urgency when their eyes met.

She'd swept her hair on top of her head, revealing the lovely stem of her neck. As he was coming to learn, every style suited her. The pink earrings still winked at him. His gaze fell lower. He knew there was a bathing suit underneath the short, wispy beach jacket covering her shapely body. It was hard not to stare at her elegant legs, half covered by the towel she was holding.

"I'm glad you suggested this, Leon. Like you, I'm anxious for some exercise before I lose it. Let's go."

*Lose it* was right. Dante's behavior at the table had cut like a knife.

Together they descended the steps to the sand. She removed her jacket and threw it on top of her towel before running into the water. He caught only a glimpse of the mini print blue-and-white bikini, but with her in it he felt a rise in his own body temperature despite the sorrow weighing him down.

"The sea feels like a bathtub," she cried in delight while treading water. He decided it had been a good idea to come out here. They both needed the distraction. Her dark sapphire eyes dazzled him with light.

He swam closer. "You've come to Rimini when the temperature is in the eighties."

"No wonder the city is a magnet for beach lovers. This is heaven!" For the next hour she kept her pain hidden. While she bobbed and dived, he swam lazy circles around her.

Leon held back bringing up the obvious until they'd left the water and stretched out on their towels. He lay on his stomach so he could look at her. She'd done the same. Belle had no idea how much her innate modesty appealed to him. It didn't matter how ruthlessly he tried to find things about her he didn't like in order to fight his attraction. He couldn't come up with one.

"What's going on in that intelligent mind of yours?"

"Flattery will get you nowhere," she said in a dampening voice, "especially when we both know you've been able to read me like a book so far."

He turned on his side. "Not this time."

She let out a troubled sigh. "I learned a lot after living with Cliff for those eight years. Whether justified or not, he felt betrayed by his parents. The family should have gotten professional counseling to help him. When I saw Dante's expression, he reminded me so much of Cliff, I got a pain in my stomach."

"The news definitely shook him."

"It was more than that, Leon." Slowly she sat up and looped her arms around her raised knees. "All I saw was the little boy who a long time ago fell apart at the loss of his mother. Your father said he's a grown man now, with a wife, and can handle it, but I'm afraid Dante's world has come crashing down on him again."

Leon nodded slowly. "If I don't miss my guess, his turmoil came from the fact that Papà wants to adopt you. Call it jealousy if you like. He and I suffered a great deal in our youth over his remarriage."

"Now he's reliving it. He sees how devoted your father is to my mother. When he said he planned to adopt me, maybe you couldn't see Dante clearly from where you were sitting, but his face went white."

"I noticed," Leon muttered. "There's no question her sin of omission has caught up with my brother."

In that moment he'd realized Dante had disliked Luciana perhaps even more strongly than Leon himself had years ago. But Dante had held back his feelings until this morning, when she'd revealed news about her secret baby. To make it even more painful, Belle had been sitting next to her mother at the table, bigger than life and more beautiful.

"I can see only one way to stop the bleeding."

Her thoughts were no longer a mystery. He rolled next to her and grasped her upper arms. "You can't go home yet—"

That nerve in her throat was throbbing again. "I have to. Don't you see? As long as I'm in Rimini, I'm a horrible reminder of his past. Mom and I have the rest of our lives to work things out. I have a career, Leon. In a few days I'll be back at my job. She can fly to New York and visit me. If I leave, then there'll be no gossip, and Mom's secret will remain safe."

His jaw hardened. "There are two flaws in your argument. In the first place the damage has already been done to Dante. Secondly, now that you've been united with her, she won't be able to handle a long-distance relationship. I've already learned enough to know a visit once every six weeks will never be enough for you, either. You can forget going anywhere," he declared.

Her chin trembled. He had the intense desire to kiss her mouth and body, but sensing danger, she eased away from him and got to her feet. "To remain in Italy for any length of time is out of the question. Don't you see it will tear Dante apart? It's not fair to him! He didn't ask for this. None of you did, but he's the one at risk of being unable to recover."

Leon stood in turn. "He'll recover, Belle, but it's going to take time."

"I don't know. I keep seeing his face and it wounds me. I have to leave. As for the rest of this week, I couldn't possibly stay at the palazzo while I'm here. That's always been Dante's home. My only option is to fly back to New York ASAP."

"No. For the time being you're going to stay with me, where you'll be away from Dante and yet still remain close to Luciana."

A small cry escaped Belle's throat. She shook her head. "I...couldn't possibly remain with you, and you know why. If I stay anywhere, it will be at a hotel."

Before he could think, she backed away

farther. In a flash she'd gathered up her jacket and towel and darted across the sand to the steps leading to the villa.

Long after she'd disappeared inside, Leon was still standing there trying to deal with a tumult of emotions regarding his brother. But he also had been gripped by unassuaged longings, and realized he had a serious problem on his hands.

Just now he'd wanted to kiss Belle into oblivion. The chemistry had been potent from the first moment they'd met. Though Benedetta hadn't been gone that long, Leon found an insidious attraction for Luciana's daughter heating up within him.

*Like father, like son?*

Something warned him it could be fatal. How was that possible? If she'd sensed it, too, that could be the reason she'd run like hell.

# CHAPTER SIX

IN A PANIC over feelings completely new to her, Belle raced to her room and jumped in the shower to wash her hair. In getting what she'd wished for by finding her mother, her world and everyone else's had been turned upside down. Nothing would ever be the same again and it was *her* fault!

Since she turned eighteen she'd been leading her own life as a liberated adult, in charge of herself and her decisions. No matter the situation now, she refused to be a weight around Leon's neck.

Her roommates would tell her she was stark staring crazy to run from the situation. They'd kill for the chance to stay with a gorgeous widower in his fabulous Italian villa. What was her problem?

Belle could only shake her head. What *wasn't* her problem? When Leon had driven her away from the palazzo earlier, she'd left it in an emotional shambles. After trying so hard not to hurt anyone, she found out that every life inside those walls standing for hundreds of years had been changed because of her driving need to know who she was.

*Are you happy now, Belle?*

In a matter of minutes Dante's life had been turned into a nightmare. She couldn't live with herself if something drastic wasn't done to staunch the flow of pain for him.

But she couldn't stay with Leon any longer, either. Through an accident of marriage, he was her *stepbrother,* for heaven's sake! Yet she had to face the awful truth that her feelings for him were anything but sisterly. She could be arrested for some of the thoughts she'd been having about him.

Just now on the beach, the ache for him had grown so acute she'd literally melted when he'd grasped her arms. It wouldn't be possible to stay with him any longer and not act on her feelings for him.

She finished blow-drying her hair and slipped on the only pair of jeans she'd brought, along with a khaki blouse. It was time to play tourist while she decided what she was going to do.

Before leaving the room in her sneakers and shoulder bag, Belle dashed off a note, which she propped on the dresser. In it she explained she'd gone for a walk and would be back later.

No one was about as she retraced her steps to the beach. It was the only way to leave his gated property. She hurried past a lifeguard tower. For all she knew, the guy on watch was one of Leon's security people. But she wouldn't worry about that now, because she'd reached the crowded public part of the beach. From there she entered one of the hotels.

After taking a couple of free pamphlets printed in English from the lobby, she walked out in front to get a taxi. She told the driver where she wanted to go. In a few minutes he dropped her off at the ancient Tiberius Bridge.

The leaflet said it was begun by the Emperor Augustus in AD 14, and completed under Tiberius in AD 21. It was a magnificent structure of five arches resting on massive pillars. Incredible to think that she was here in such a historic place, but she couldn't appreciate it.

Tormented because she didn't know what she should do, Belle crossed the river to the city center to window-shop and eat a late lunch. The brochure indicated the Piazza Cavour was once the area of the fish and vegetable markets during the Middle Ages.

It was fascinating information, but partway through her meal she lost interest in her food. Sightseeing hadn't been a good idea and there were too many tourists. She decided to find a taxi and return to the villa. As she got up from the table, she almost bumped into Leon, who was pushing Concetta in her baby stroller.

"Leon!" Belle cried in utter surprise. The sight of his tall, powerful body clothed in jeans and a white polo shirt took her breath. "Where did you come from?"

A seductive smile broke out on his firm lips. Her gaze traveled to the cleft in his chin. The enticing combination was too much for her. "We've been following you."

Belle might have known Leon's security people would keep him informed of her every step. In spite of knowing she'd been watched and followed, a rush of warmth invaded her. To offset it, she knelt down to give the baby kisses. "So *that's* what you've been doing. Are you having a wonderful time?"

Concetta kept smiling at her as if she really recognized her and was happy to see her. That sweet little face had a lock on Belle's emotions.

"When we found your note, we thought we'd join you."

*No*... To spend more time with him and the baby wasn't a good idea. "I was just going to find a taxi and go back."

"Fine. My car is parked right over there on the side street."

Caving to the inevitable, Belle said, "May I push her?"

"Go ahead, but you'll have to dodge the heavy foot traffic."

She rubbed her hand over Concetta's fine hair. "We don't mind, do we, sweetheart."

As they navigated through the crowds toward his car, every woman in sight feasted her eyes on Leon. His black hair and striking looks compelled them to stare. Belle felt their envy when they glanced at her. She had to admit that if she'd been a tourist and had seen him with his little girl, she would have found him irresistible. There was nothing that captured a female's attention faster than an attractive man out with his baby and enjoying it, especially this one.

"On the way home we'll stop by the Delfinario."

"That's an intriguing word."

With half-veiled eyes, he helped her and

Concetta into the backseat of the sedan. "I think you'll be entertained."

"Is it animal, vegetable or mineral?"

Leon burst into rich laughter. "You'll get your answer before long."

Her heart went into flutter mode, something that had started happening only since she'd been in Leon's company.

He drove along the beach until they came to what appeared to be a theme park. After they got out he said, "I'll carry Concetta. Come with me."

Belle followed him to a large, open-air pool. She spotted some mammals leaping out of the water. "Dolphins?"

*"Sì, signorina. Delfino."* Leon paid the admission and found them two seats in the packed arena where they were performing. Belle could pick out a few familiar words spoken by the man narrating the show in Italian. She loved the sound of the language. The children in the audience were enraptured by the sight.

"Look, Concetta!" Belle pointed to them. "Can you see the *delfino?*"

The baby got caught up in the excitement and clapped her hands like the kids surrounding them. More enchanted by her reaction than by the remarkable tricks happening in the water with the trainers, both Leon and Belle laughed with abandon.

After one spectacular feat, their eyes met and she flashed him a full, unguarded smile. Belle found it impossible to hold back her enjoyment in being here like this with the two of them, as if they were a family. It wasn't until later, on their drive home, that she was brought back to reality, knowing she had a huge decision to make.

"I think my little *tesoro* needs her dinner."

"Would you let me feed her and put her to bed?" Being with the baby brought Belle comfort, the kind she needed right now.

"Of course. It will give Talia a break."

"Oh goody. Did you hear that, Concetta?" Belle was sitting next to her in the back of the sedan and kissed her half a dozen times.

Once they arrived at the villa, Leon carried her in the kitchen to her high chair and got out the baby food for Belle. Another fun-filled half hour passed while the child ate and played with her food, smearing some of it on the traytop as well as herself.

Laughter rumbled out of Leon. "I had no idea she could be this messy an eater."

"Most babies make a huge mess when you make a game out of eating. She's so happy. Look at the way she beams at you, Leon. It's the cutest thing I ever saw. But let's be honest. She's in need of a bath big-time."

"You took the words out of my mouth. Her little plastic tub is under the sink in the bathroom."

"I'll get everything set up." As Belle turned to leave the room, Concetta started to cry, causing Belle to turn around. "Oh, sweetie, I'm just going upstairs."

Leon darted her a piercing glance while he cleaned the baby off. "My daughter is already so crazy about you, she's not going to want Talia's attention."

Belle's heart thudded. "I hope that's not true," she whispered. "See you in a minute, Concetta." She hurried through the house and up the stairs to the nursery. Once she'd started filling the tub, she found the baby shampoo and a towel.

"Leon?" she called out. "Everything's ready!"

"Here we come!" He breezed into the bathroom, carrying his daughter in the altogether and lowering her into the water. Concetta talked her head off and splashed water everywhere.

"Already you're a water baby, aren't you, sweetheart? That's a good thing, because you've got a swimming pool and the Adriatic right in your own backyard." Leon grinned as he poured a little shampoo on her head.

Belle massaged it in. "Are you having fun, my little brown-eyed Susan?"

"What's that?" Leon asked. His command of English was remarkable, but once in a while he could be surprised.

"A yellow flower like a daisy with a center just like her incredible eyes."

He nodded. "The first time I looked into them, they reminded me of poppy throats."

Spoken like a father in love with his little offshoot. "They're both apt descriptions. One day she's going to grow up and drive all the Rimini *ragazzi* wild."

A burst of laughter broke from his throat. "Your knowledge of Italian is impressive. But let's hope that eventuality is years away yet."

"I don't know. They grow up fast." Belle kissed the baby's neck. "Are you having fun, sweetheart? I know *I* am." Truly, she'd never had so much fun in her life.

"That makes two of us," Leon said in his deep voice.

He made a wonderful father. If every child could be so lucky...

Once the bath was over, she slipped a diaper on Concetta and Leon found a light green sleeper. "Here's the bottle." He handed it to her. "Would you like to give it to her?"

"You know I would."

Belle sat down in the rocker with the baby and sang to her. So much playtime had made Concetta sleepy. Her eyelids drooped almost at once while she drank her formula. The long lashes reminded Belle of Leon's. Before long the child stopped sucking and fell sound asleep.

Leon watched as Belle put the baby down in the crib on her back. After they'd left the nursery he turned to her.

"Now that we've got the evening to ourselves, I'm taking you out on the cabin cruiser so you can get a view of the coast from the water. It's a sight you shouldn't miss. The pier is a few steps down the beach, in the opposite direction from where you went earlier today."

"I figured the lifeguard was one of your security people, but he didn't try to stop me."

Leon's lips twitched. "While we're out, I'd like to discuss something of vital importance with you. I've worked out a solution to our problem."

"So have I." She was going home on Sunday as planned, with no interference from him.

His black brows lifted in challenge, as if

he could read her thoughts. "Then we'll compare notes," he said in an authoritative tone. His hauteur came naturally to him, because it was evident few people had ever dared thwart him. "Meet me on the back patio in twenty minutes. Bring a wrap. It will get cool later."

She nodded before hurrying downstairs to her room. She couldn't imagine what kind of solution he'd worked out, and didn't want to listen to him, not when Dante's happiness was at stake. But she was a guest in Leon's home and couldn't forget her debt to him. It was one she could never repay.

Without him acting on his uncanny instinct to follow through on her inquiry at the bank, she would have gone on searching for her mother in vain. The situation was untenable any way she looked at it.

A tap on the door a few minutes later brought her head around. *"Signorina?"* Belle rushed over to open it and discovered Carla. "The Countess Malatesta phoned while you were bathing the baby. She would like you to call her." The maid handed Belle a note with the phone number written on it.

"Thank you, Carla."

After she left, Belle pulled the cell phone

out of her purse and called her mother. Two rings and she answered. "Arabella?"

It was still unbelievable to Belle that she was talking to the mother she'd ached for all her life. "Mom—I'm so glad you called. To hear your voice…it's like a miracle to me."

"I was just going to tell you the same thing, darling. What have you done with your day?"

Belle bit her lip. "I went sightseeing and Leon took me and the baby to see the dolphins. Then we fed her and bathed her. Now she's just gone to sleep." But Belle didn't want to talk about Leon and the way he made her feel. Her mouth had gone so dry thinking about him, she could hardly swallow. "How's Dante? I've been worried sick about him."

"To be truthful, we've been worried, too. They've stayed in their wing of the palazzo all day. Since they have their own entrance, they could have gone out without our knowing it. Sullisto and I thought we'd done the right thing to tell him the truth this morning…" Her voice trailed off. "I know my husband's hurt by this."

Belle gripped the phone tighter. "If it's any consolation, I don't think it would have mattered when you told Dante. The outcome would be the same. Maybe tonight he'll decide to talk to you, so I'm not planning to come over. Can we see each other tomorrow?"

"That's why I phoned you. I'll pick you up in the morning and we'll take a drive. I want to show you my world. We'll talk and eat our heads off. How does that sound?"

She smiled. "Like heaven."

"Let's say eight-thirty."

"Perfect. I'll be ready. I love you, Mom."

"I love *you*. Isn't it wonderful to be able to say it to each other?"

"Yes." *Oh yes.*

After they hung up, Belle threw herself across the bed and thought about the day Cliff had let her know she wasn't wanted or loved.

She'd been a child then, with a child's reaction. But she was a woman now, and understood Cliff's behavior, just as she understood Dante's. In both cases Belle had been the one to bring on more suffering. This time she had the power to end it.

When it was time to meet Leon, she grabbed her sweater and hurried down to the patio. She would listen to what he had to say, but it wouldn't change her mind about leaving on Sunday.

*  *  *

Leon knew something was up the minute he saw her. "What's happened since you went downstairs?" he asked as they headed for the dock.

"I just got off the phone with Mom. They haven't seen Dante all day."

"My father told me the same thing a few minutes ago, but it isn't surprising. His way is to hide out."

"What do you mean, *his* way?"

Leon sobered. "There are things you don't know."

She took a shuddering breath. "Well, I know one thing. My arrival in Rimini has hurt him."

"It's not personal, Belle. *I'm* the one who has hurt him."

Her brows met in a frown as she looked at him. "How can you say that?"

"Because it's true. You saw and heard what happened at the table when Father said I was the one who made the reunion possible. Dante couldn't handle it and blew up at me in Italian."

She shook her head. "The whole thing is tragic. Mom's going to take me for a drive tomorrow. Maybe if Dante knows she's out of the palazzo, he and your father will be able to talk."

"I don't think so."

"Why do you sound so sure about that?"

"Once we're on board, I'll explain." Leon couldn't let Belle go on thinking she was the cause of everything.

He helped her climb over the side of the cruiser. After giving her a life jacket to put on, he undid the ropes and started the engine. They moved at a wakeless speed until they were past the drop-off before he opened it up.

She knelt on the bench across from the captain's seat, looking out to sea. "Is it always this placid?"

"It is this time of evening. Much later a breeze will spring up."

"You weren't exaggerating about the view. With the blue changing into darkness, all the lights twinkling along the shoreline make everything magical."

"Your eyes are the same color right now. Twilight eyes."

His words seemed to disturb her, because she turned around to face him. "You said you would tell me about Dante. Let's talk about him." She was a businesswoman who'd been fending off men's advances for years and knew how to probe through to the marrow.

He shut off the engine and lowered the anchor. After turning to her, he extended his legs. "When Dante and I lost our mother to cancer, he was ten and I eleven. For several years we were pretty inconsolable. Father had always been so preoccupied with business, she was the one who played with us and made life exciting. No one could be more fun. We could go to her with any problem and she'd fix it."

"You were blessed to have her that long."

"We were, but at the time all we could realize was that her death left a great void. Sometimes Benedetta saw me walking on the grounds and she'd join me with her dog. She wouldn't say anything, but she was a comfort, and I found myself unburdening to her the way kids do. Unfortunately, Dante didn't have that kind of a confidante. All he had was me, and I was a poor substitute."

"Don't say that, Leon. Just having a sibling, knowing you're there, makes such a difference. There were several siblings at the orphanage. They had a special bond without even talking. If you could discuss this with Dante, I'm sure he would tell you how much it meant to have a brother who understood what he was going through."

Leon studied her for a moment. "You have so much insight, Belle, there are times when I'm a little in awe of you. But you haven't heard everything yet."

She smiled sadly. "I was the great observer of life, don't forget. You've seen people like me before. We hover at the top of the staircase, watching everyone below, never being a part of things. But I eventually grew out of my self-pity. I had to!"

"Look at you now, a successful businesswoman."

Belle leaned forward. "What happened to your relationship with Dante? I want to know. Was it terrible when your father told you boys he was getting married again?" The compassion in her eyes was tangible.

"The truth?" She nodded. "We both felt betrayed."

"You poor things."

"To be honest, I couldn't fathom him marrying anyone else. Our mom was a motherly sort, the perfect mother, if you know what I mean. She made everything fun, always laughing and lively, always there for us.

"Her death brought a pall over our household. Dante came to my room every night and cried his heart out. I had to hold back my tears to try and help him."

"That's so sad, Leon. I believe the heartache you two endured had to be worse than anything I ever experienced at the orphanage. To be so happy with your mother, and then have her gone…"

He sucked in his breath. "Things got worse when Papà brought Luciana to the palazzo to meet us. The diamond heiress looked young enough to be his daughter. In fact, she didn't look old enough to be anyone's mother. I found her cool and remote."

Belle's heart twisted. "I can't picture her that way."

"That's because meeting you has changed her into a different person. At the time I hated her for being so beautiful. Anyone could see why she'd attracted our father. As you heard through the librarian, there'd been rumors that both Luciana's mother and her widowed father might have been murdered."

Belle nodded.

"Some of those rumors linked my father to the latter possible crime. I knew in my heart Papà couldn't have done such a thing, but I was filled with anger."

"Why exactly?"

"Because I was old enough to understand

that love had nothing to do with his marriage to her. He'd done what all Malatestas had done before him, and reached out to bring the Donatello diamond fortune under the far-reaching umbrella of our family's assets.

"Gossip was rife at the time. People were waiting to see if he produced another heir. It felt like he'd betrayed our mother, and I couldn't forgive him. Dante felt the same way and threatened to run away."

"How terrible," Belle whispered sadly.

"I told him we couldn't do that. But when we turned eighteen, we would leave. Until then we had to go along with things and deal with the ugly rumors surrounding the Donatello family. But I let him down when I made the decision to go away to college."

"You had to live your own life."

He raked his hair back absently. "This morning's explosion lets me know I made a big mistake in leaving." Pain stabbed his insides, forcing him to his feet.

"What do you mean?"

"I left Dante on his own to deal with his pain. I should have stayed and helped him, but I didn't. Papà's marriage to a princess shrouded in gossip and mystery was so distasteful to me, I couldn't get out of the palazzo fast enough. I could have gone to college in Rimini, but instead I went to Rome in order to get away.

"During the years I was gone, Dante's pain turned to anger. When I returned, he was involved with his own friends. I moved to the villa, one of the properties I inherited from our mother's estate, and dug into business at the bank. Later on I began to spend more time with Benedetta. My brother and I had grown apart, but that was my fault."

Belle put a hand on his arm. At the first contact, tiny sensations of delight he couldn't ward off spread through his body. "You couldn't help what happened then," she murmured.

Leon looked down at her hand. "Oh yes, I could have, but I was too caught up in my own pain to reach out. Dante didn't display any outward signs of rebellion, but obviously, he was riddled with turmoil once our father's marriage was a fait accompli. I didn't see it manifested until I came home from college."

"Didn't your father try to prepare you for his marriage to my mother?"

"No, but to be honest, if he *had* tried, it wouldn't have done any good. Be assured I'll always love my father, but there was a gulf between us. While I was gone I stayed in touch with him and Dante, even made a few short visits on holidays. But it was four years later before I returned to Rimini to live.

"By that time Dante no longer shared his innermost thoughts with me. The closeness we once enjoyed seemed to have vanished for good. I'm afraid that for him, it was a hurt that never went away.

"He married Pia Rovere, a distant relative from our mother's side of the family. They chose to live in another wing of the Malatesta palazzo. That arrangement pleased my father and suited me, since I preferred living on my own at the villa."

"She's lovely."

"And very good for Dante, I think. Since then the three of us work in the family banking business. Unfortunately, the relations between my father and me continue to be frayed because of my marriage to Benedetta."

Belle's delicately arched brows met. "I don't understand."

"When I married her, I did something no other Malatesta has done, and took a woman without a title for my wife. I made it clear I wanted nothing to do with such an archaic custom. My father has had no choice but to look to Dante to follow in his footsteps."

"Which he has done by marrying Pia, who's from a royal house."

Again Leon frowned. "But now that Benedetta is gone, Papà is counting on my marrying a titled woman he has in mind to be Concetta's new mother. He's made no secret about it. Every time he brings it up in front of Dante, which is often, I keep reminding him that even if I weren't in mourning, I would never do as he wants. I've told him I'm not interested in marriage and only want to be a good father to my daughter."

Belle let out a troubled sigh. "Why do you think he's so intent on it?"

"Because I'm the firstborn son and the firstborn is supposed to inherit the title."

"In other words, he would prefer you to receive it over Dante."

"Yes. It isn't that he loves Dante less, but he's a stickler for duty. Luciana's father was of that same ilk. It's the one area where Father and I don't get along."

"I'm surprised he didn't forbid you to marry Benedetta."

"He did, but we got married in a private ceremony before he knew about it, and his hands were tied."

Belle studied him for a minute. "I'm sure

you must miss your wife terribly. Tell me about her."

"I knew her from childhood. She was Dante's age. Our mother was an animal lover. We spent hours at the kennel playing with the dogs. Benedetta was always there, helping her father. She'd lost her mother to pneumonia, and our mom took her under her wing. It was like having a sister."

"So your love for her was based on long-standing friendship first."

He nodded. "It wasn't until several years after I returned from Rome that my feelings for her underwent a change."

"What happened?"

"She worked for her father and had a Spinone who'd been her devoted pet for a long time. I happened to be at the palazzo one day in the fall when word came to us that her dog was missing. I knew how much she loved him, so I gathered some staff to go look for him. We found him shot dead by a hunter we presumed had trespassed on the property."

"What a dreadful thing to happen. I can't bear it."

"Neither could I. When I saw him lying there, I felt like I'd been the one who'd received the bullet. Benedetta was so heartbroken, I didn't think she'd recover. I dropped everything to be with her for the next week. We comforted each other. She'd always had a sweetness that drew me to her."

"You must have had a wonderful marriage."

"For the short time we were given, I was the happiest I'd ever been."

Leon heard Belle take a deep breath. "One day your daughter is going to love hearing about your love story." After a slight hesitation, she added, "How hard for both of you to find out she had that disease. What was it like? I hope you don't mind my asking."

For the first time since it happened, Leon felt like talking about it. "At first she grew very tired, and then suffered some hair loss. I came home from the office early many times to be with her, console her. After a while she couldn't go out in the sun. As time passed, more symptoms occurred. She had painful swollen joints and fever, even kidney problems."

"That must have been so awful, Leon."

"I didn't want to believe it would get worse. We prayed she'd get it under control, and were both looking forward to the baby. I never dreamed I'd lose her during the delivery. I was in shock for days."

"Of course. I'm so sorry. Did she suffer a long time?"

"No, *grazie a Dio.*"

"Then you received two blessings, one of them being your adorable daughter." Belle shifted position and lowered her head. "How did you cope with a newborn?"

"You've met Simona and Talia. They worked for my mother's family and I trusted them implicitly. They fell in love with the baby and have been with me ever since. I couldn't have made it without them."

"Did your father help?"

"Yes. Everyone did what they could. Their love for Concetta brought us all a little closer together."

"Then you'd think that after a marriage like yours, and that sweet baby, your father would give up his futile desire and leave you alone to decide what you want from life."

Leon nodded. "That's what a normal parent would do. Perhaps now you're beginning to understand what I've always been up against. The point is, I would never choose a woman of rank."

"Why do you feel so strongly about it? I'm curious."

"My parents were officially betrothed before they ever met each other. They made their arranged marriage work. From what I saw, they were kind and decent to each other, sometimes showing each other affection. But until Mother was dying, I didn't know she'd loved another man and had to give him up."

*His mother had told him something else, too.*

"I can't begin to imagine it," Belle was saying.

"After realizing the sacrifice she'd made to marry for duty, I made up my mind that her situation wasn't going to happen to me. When the time came, I proposed to Benedetta without hesitation."

Belle shifted restlessly in her seat. "I guess that meant your father had to sacrifice, too."

Leon nodded. "You know what's interesting? The other night Father told me that when he asked Luciana to marry him, he said, 'Naturally, it wasn't like the feelings I had for your mother, but then you can't expect that.'"

"So what do you think he was really saying?"

"That he was still trying to protect me by pretending he'd loved our mother, but I knew it wasn't true. They were never in love with each other. Do you want to know something else?"

Her eyes fastened on him, revealing her concern in the reflection of the cruiser's lights.

"I think the real truth is he fell deeply in

love with Luciana, enough to overlook everything in order to make her his wife."

After a slight hesitation, Belle said, "I'm pretty sure she has learned to love him, too. The way she talked to him at the table convinces me they are very close."

"So close, in fact, he wants to adopt you to make her completely happy."

"He mustn't do that..." Her features screwed up in pain. "Think of the damage it would do to Dante. I can't handle that. You've got to stop him, Leon!"

Her reaction was even more than he'd hoped for. "I agree, and I've thought of a foolproof plan. I failed my brother when I went away to college in Rome, but this will be a way to atone for my sins."

"What can you do?" she cried. "Tell me."

"It involves your cooperation, but it has to be so convincing to everyone, and I mean *everyone,* no one will believe it's not true."

Determination filled her gaze. "I'll do anything."

"I hope you mean that."

"I swear it. Since Dante left the table, I've been dying inside."

Leon reached out to squeeze her hand before letting it go. "First you have to phone your boss and tell him you need to take family leave. Let him know you're in Italy visiting the mother you were just reunited with. Tell him an emergency has arisen that prevents you from returning to work Monday. They have to give you the time off."

Leon heard her take several short breaths in succession. "I…suppose that could be arranged, especially when I've never asked for it before."

*"Bene."* He checked his watch. "Now would be the perfect time to reach him at work." He handed her his phone. "Once you've talked to him, you'll be able to concentrate on our plan."

"I don't know what it is yet."

"Before I say anything else, we need to know if everything's all right for you to stay in Rimini. If not, I'll have to come up with another plan. While you do that, we'll head back to shore."

He raised anchor and started the engine. The sound prevented him from hearing much of her conversation. By the time they reached the dock, she'd finished the call. While he tied up the cruiser, he gave her a covert glance. "What's the verdict?"

"I couldn't believe he was so nice. He said for me to take all the time I needed. Not to worry."

*"Eccelente."*
*One roadblock removed.*

Belle handed him the phone and took off her life jacket, which he stowed away under the bench. She replaced it with her sweater. "When are you going to tell me the plan?"

"I don't know about you, but I could use some coffee. Let's go up to the villa and check on Concetta. Then we'll have the rest of the night to talk everything out."

"I admit coffee sounds good. It's getting cooler."

He helped Belle step onto the dock and they made their way back in silence. They might not be touching, but the sensual tension between them was palpable. Talia saw them in the hall and told him Concetta was sleeping like an angel.

Before heading for the kitchen, he and Belle went upstairs and tiptoed into the nursery to take a peek. Suddenly, both of them chuckled, because the baby was sitting up in the crib. She saw them in the doorway and started fussing.

"It looks like she was waiting for you to say good-night," Belle whispered. Leon crossed the room to pick her up and hug her. His heart dissolved when his child kissed him and patted his cheeks. "She adores you, Leon."

The sound of her voice brought his daughter's head around. To their surprise she reached for Belle, who caught her in her arms.

"Are you going to give me a kiss goodnight, too? How lucky can I be? I love you, sweetheart." She walked her around the room. "I wish Concetta knew what I was saying, Leon."

"She doesn't need to understand English to know what you mean," he murmured in a satisfied voice.

"Is that true?" Belle kissed her again.

In the intimacy of the darkened room his daughter clung to her as if she were her mother. It added substance to an idea that had been building in his mind since the first time Belle had picked her up.

He'd planned to talk to her after they'd gone back downstairs for coffee, but his little girl had unexpectedly chosen the place and the moment for this conversation.

"Since she's not ready to go to sleep yet, I'll tell you my plan now. We need to get married right away to prevent my father from adopting you."

# CHAPTER SEVEN

BELLE LET OUT a laugh that filled the nursery. She stood in front of Leon with the baby's head nestled against her neck. "Right away? As in…"

"Tomorrow."

"I didn't know it was possible," she mocked.

"I have a friend in high places."

"Naturally. So *that's* the solution to all our problems? From the man who's still grieving for his wife and never intends to marry again?"

Leon couldn't help smiling. "It's even stranger, considering that I've proposed to a woman who has declared marriage isn't an option for her."

Belle patted Concetta's back. "All right. Now that you've gotten my attention, let's hear what's really on your mind."

"You just heard it."

"Be serious, Leon."

He shifted his weight. "When you allow it to sink in, you'll discover it makes perfect sense. Our marriage will make it unnecessary for the adoption to take place, because you'll be my wife, mistress of our household, mother to my child."

His words caused Belle to clutch his little girl tighter.

"Concetta's tiny eyelids are fluttering, on the verge of sleep. That's how comfortable she is with you. She needs a mother, Belle. I've been blind to that reality for a long time. But seeing her with you is so right. Just now I heard you tell her you loved her. That came from your heart, so don't deny it."

Belle could hardly swallow. "I'm not denying it."

"If we marry, there'll be two desired outcomes, both of them critical. First, our marriage will enable you to have the full relationship you deserve with your mother for the rest of your lives, without moving into the palazzo. We both know that's Dante's territory and should remain so."

She hugged the baby closer.

"Secondly, it will prevent any more machinations on my father's part to see me married to the titled woman he's picked out for me. After all, who could be a more fitting bride than his wife's daughter? The beauty of it is that I'll be the one who takes care of you, not my father."

In a furtive movement, Belle walked over to the crib and tried to put the baby down. But Concetta wasn't having any of it and started crying again, so she picked her back up. "You need to go to sleep, little love."

A satisfied smile curled Leon's lips. "She doesn't want to leave your arms. It convinces me my daughter has bonded with you in a way she hasn't done with anyone else but me. You have to realize how important that is to me. She's been my world since Benedetta died."

"I'm very much aware of that."

"When I told Father I would never marry again, I meant it at the time. How could I ever find a woman who would be the kind of mother to Concetta that my mother was to me and Dante? But your arrival in Rimini has changed all that."

Belle buried her face in the baby's neck to shield herself from his words.

"Tonight I watched my daughter reach for you. With the evidence before my eyes, I know that with you as my wife, she'll have a mother who will always love her. I *know* how much you care for her already. I've seen the way you respond to her. It's the same way Luciana responds. Like mother, like daughter."

Belle kissed the little girl's head. "As long as we're having this absurd conversation, there's one thing you haven't mentioned."

"You're talking about love, of course. Since we both made a conscious decision not to marry, before we met, we won't have that expectation. But there's desire between us, as we found out yesterday. Which is vital for any marriage.

"Furthermore, we've become friends, who both love our families. Between us we can turn all the negatives into a positive, in order for you to be with your mother and calm Dante's fears." Leon moved closer. "Nothing has to change for you. Talia will continue to be Concetta's nanny. If the bank backs a new TCCPI outlet in Rimini, you'll be installed as the manager and can go on working."

"I guess it doesn't surprise me you could make that happen," she muttered.

"Let me make myself clear. I'd do *anything* to give my daughter a life that includes a mother and a father." Leon's voice grated. "Your journey to Italy to find your mother has convinced me you'd do anything to be close to her. If a career you've carved out for yourself will keep you here, then you can be a mother, have your career and stay near Luciana. Won't that be worth it to you?"

Belle shook her head. "I can't believe we're having this conversation. But for the sake of argument, what you're suggesting is that we enter into an arranged marriage."

He reached for Concetta and put her back in the crib. This time she didn't cry, but she held on to his finger. "Yes, but one in which we haven't been pressured by anyone. I realize I can't compete with your roommates for the companionship you enjoy with them, but I'm not so bad. We had fun watching the dolphins, didn't we?"

"That question doesn't require a response. What you're suggesting is ludicrous."

"Now you have some idea of how my parents must have felt when they had to enter into an arranged marriage. At least with you and me, we've both felt the fire. How long it lasts is anyone's guess. But if nothing I've said has made any difference in how you feel, then it appears the only alternative is for you to go back to your life in New York."

*What life was that?*

Leon lifted his head to appraise her. "While I stay with Concetta until she's asleep, why don't you go down to the kitchen and have that coffee you wanted? I'll join you shortly and you can give me your definitive answer."

"You think it's that simple?"

He grimaced. "No. I only know that we can't change what has happened, and a decision has to be made one way or the other."

"Like I said, I shouldn't have come to Italy."

"It's too late for regrets, and we've already had this conversation. The only thing to do is move forward. Just be aware that whether you stay here or go back to the States, my father plans to adopt you. He's been so eager to do it, only time will tell how that hurt has affected Dante. His relationship with our father and Luciana has been rocky at times."

"I don't want him hurt."

"Neither do I." Leon lifted his brows. "If you can think of a better way than marriage to prevent more pain from happening and still be close to your mother, I'll be the first one to listen."

"I'll go to your father and beg him not to do anything."

"It won't do you any good, Belle. On certain issues, my father is adamant. Where your mother is concerned, this is the gift he wants to give her, and no amount of tears or cajoling will change his mind."

"Not even for Dante's sake?"

"I'm afraid not. You heard my father. Dante's a grown man and should be able to handle it."

Belle was frantic. "You can't really mean what you've been saying…"

"Why do you think I married Benedetta in the dark of night?" he countered.

Belle's head jerked back. "But it's a feudal system!"

"I've been fighting it all my life."

At this point she was pacing the floor. Finally she stopped and turned to him. "What would we tell our parents? We've known each other only a few days."

"We'll tell them it was love at first sight. They won't be able to say anything. I happen to know Papà fell for Luciana the minute he met her. He'd never known a love like that with my mother."

Belle pressed her lips together. "It's so sad about your parents."

"They managed, but it's past history now. I can't speak for Luciana, but she must have had strong feelings for my father in order to get married again so soon after losing the man she'd first loved."

"You're really serious about this, aren't you."

"Serious enough that I've been on the phone with our old family priest, who married everyone in our family. He stands ready with a special license to officiate at the church tomorrow morning. All you'll need to provide is your passport. My staff will be our witnesses."

Belle stared blindly into space. "I was supposed to go out for the day with Mom...."

"Call her and tell her there's been a change in plans. Promise her I'll drive you to the palazzo later in the morning. When we arrive with Concetta, hopefully Dante and Pia will be there, so we can make the announcement of our nuptials in front of everyone."

"You don't just get married like this—"

"Most normal people don't. But we happened to be born to a mother and father with unique birthrights, who are married to each other, thus complicating your life and mine. With our marriage taking place, the idea of my father wanting to adopt you will fade, and take the sword out of Dante's hand. It might even improve our relationship. Much more than that, I can't promise. Only time will tell."

Belle edged away from him. "This is all moving too fast."

"The situation demands action. Father believes you're going back to New York on Sunday. When he announced he was planning to adopt you, I knew it meant he'd already been in touch with his attorney. He'll want your signature on the adoption papers before you leave. When he makes a decision, he acts on it before you can blink."

"You're a lot like him."

"Is that a good or a bad thing?"

"Please don't joke at a time like this, Leon."

Concetta had finally fallen asleep. He walked across the room to Belle. Reaching in his pocket, he pulled out a ring. She stared at the plain gold band. "What are you doing?"

He took her left hand in his. "Your engagement ring. Tomorrow it will be the wedding ring of Signora Arabella Donatello Sloan di Malatesta."

Belle pulled her hand away before he could put it on her. "I haven't agreed to anything."

He stared at her through shuttered eyes. "Then in the morning all you have to do is tell me you don't want it, and we won't talk of it again."

"Leon—you can't do this to me!"

"Do what? Offer to marry you so I can give you my name and protection? Help you to enjoy the mother you never knew? Give you the opportunity to be a mother to my daughter, who's already welcomed you into her life?"

"You know what I mean!" Belle cried.

"Don't you think I'd like to make up to you for the years of emotional deprivation? For the cruelty you received at your stepbrother's hands?" he demanded. "Don't you know your existence has changed destiny for all of us?"

His words scorched her. She wished to heaven she had someone to talk to. Ironically, now that she'd found her mother, she couldn't go to her. Not about this. It was worse than getting caught in the maze she'd seen earlier on the palazzo grounds.

"What do *you* get out of this?"

"I thought you understood. The most remarkable mother in the world for my daughter, and a possible chance to win back my brother's affection. When Benedetta became so ill, she begged me that one day I'd find happiness with someone else. At the time I didn't want to hear it, but she was right. Life has to go on. Our marriage will be a start along that path. Until you flew into my world, I didn't know where to begin."

Belle couldn't take any more. "I'm going to say good-night." Without hesitation she bolted from the nursery and flew down the stairs to her bedroom.

For the rest of the night she tossed and turned, going over every argument in her mind. Could she really enter into a marriage when she knew Leon's heart had died after losing his wife? Belle couldn't hope to compete with her memory, but he wasn't asking for love. He wanted her to be Concetta's mother.

It was probably the only area in Belle's life where she felt confident. If she had that little baby for her very own, she could pour out all the love she had to give. Belle could be the kind of mother to Concetta she'd dreamed of having herself.

Leon *wanted* her to be his baby's mother.

That had to mean something, didn't it?

He was the most marvelous man. To think he trusted her with his prized possession!

Even if she was a virgin who'd had no experience with men, she could do the mothering part right. Maybe their marriage would help heal the wound between Leon and his family.

Marriage to him would ensure a close relationship with Belle's mother for the rest of their lives.

But what if Leon met another woman and fell in love?

Belle knew the answer to that: it would kill her. But would their union be so different from the many marriages where one of the partners strayed? It was a fact of life that millions of married men and women had affairs. There were no guarantees.

By the time morning came, she'd gone back and forth so many times she was physically and emotionally exhausted. But one thing stood out above all else. The thought of going back to her life in New York seemed like living death....

It was a beautiful, warm summer Saturday morning for a wedding in Rimini. In a veil and a white silk and lace wedding dress of her dreams, Belle stepped out of the bridal shop with Leon. They walked to his car where her bouquet lay on the backseat. He'd thought of everything. Belle heard the church bells of San Giovanni before they arrived. Though it was much more ornate than the church attached to the orphanage in Newburgh, Belle had the same sense of homecoming once Leon ushered her inside the doors.

Church had always been her one place of comfort, whether she'd been at the orphanage or the Petersons'. Except that this morning she was to be married to the dark prince of Rimini, as she'd first thought of him. Nothing seemed real.

He'd pinned a gardenia corsage to her linen suit before they'd left the villa. In the lapel of his midnight-blue silk suit, he wore a smaller gardenia. Belle could smell the fragrance she would always associate with being a bride, but she couldn't seem to feel anything. It was as if she were standing outside her body.

Leon's staff came in a separate car. They followed them down the aisle to the shrine in front, where the old priest was waiting in his colorful vestments. Talia carried the baby, who so far was being very good, and looked adorable in a white lace dress and white sandals with pink rosettes.

The priest clasped both of Belle's hands and welcomed her with a broad smile. "Princess Arabella?" She almost fainted at being addressed that way. "You look like your mother did when I married her and the count," he explained in heavily accented

English. "Leonardo has advised that I per-
form this ceremony in English. Are you
ready?"

"We are." Leon answered for them in his
deep voice.

"If the witnesses will stand on either side."

Talia and Simona stood on Leon's right.
He kissed his daughter, who kept making
sounds. Carla stood on Belle's left.

"Arabella and Leonardo, you have come
together in this church so that the Lord may
seal and strengthen your love in the presence of the church's minister and this community. Christ abundantly blesses this love.
In the presence of the church, I ask you to
state your intentions. Have you come here
freely and without reservation to give your-
selves to each other in marriage?"

Without reservation? Belle panicked, but
she said yes after Leon's affirmative response.

"Will you love and honor each other as
man and wife for the rest of your lives?"

That wasn't as difficult to answer. Belle
did honor him. He was the one responsible
for finding her mother. And there were many
things about him she loved very much. The
way he loved his daughter melted her heart.

"Will you accept children lovingly from

God, and bring them up according to the law of Christ and His church?"

That was a question Belle hadn't been expecting. But how could she say no when she'd just admitted to coming here freely to give herself in marriage? She said a faint yes, but didn't know if the priest heard her.

"Take her hand, *figlio mio*."

Leon's grasp was warm against her cold fingers. He rubbed his thumb over her skin to get the circulation flowing. *That* she felt.

"Repeat after me. I, Leonardo Rovere di Malatesta, take you, Arabella Donatello Sloan, to be my wife. I promise to be true to you in good times and in bad, in sickness and in health. I will love you and honor you all the days of my life."

The next few moments were surreal for Belle, who could hear the words of the ceremony uttered by the priest, and their own responses. Concetta's baby talk provided a background.

Blood pounded in Belle's ears when he said, "You have declared your consent before the church. May the Lord in His goodness strengthen your consent and fill you both with His blessings. What God has joined, men must not divide. Leonardo? You have rings?"

*Oh no.* Belle didn't have one for him.

"We do."

"Lord, may these rings be a symbol of true faith in each other, and always remind them of their love, through Christ our Lord. Leonardo?"

Belle watched him pull the gold band out of his pocket. "Put it on her finger and repeat after me. Take this ring as a sign of my love and fidelity. In the name of the Father, and of the Son, and of the Holy Spirit."

It was really happening…

Leon reached in his pocket again and pulled out his signet ring to hand to her.

The priest said, "Arabella? Repeat after me. Take this ring as a sign of my love and fidelity. In the name of the Father, and of the Son, and of the Holy Spirit."

After saying the words, she was all thumbs as she put it on the ring finger of Leon's left hand. He'd removed his own wedding band. How hard that must have been, after the love he'd shared with Benedetta.

While she was still staring at his hand incredulously, Leon put a finger under her chin and tilted her head so he could kiss her.

"We've done it, Belle. You're my wife now," he whispered against her lips. "Thank you for this gift only you could have given, to help me raise Concetta. For that you will always have my undying devotion."

When his mouth covered hers, it was different from a husband's kiss. She didn't know what she'd expected, but it was more like a sweet, reverent benediction. Quickly recovering from her surprise, she whispered back, "Then we're even, because you've given me the gift of my mother and your precious daughter."

By now Concetta was making herself heard and getting wiggly. Belle saw Leon reach for her, and with a triumphant cry hug her in his strong arms.

The staff huddled around Belle with moist eyes to congratulate her. Their well-wishing was so genuine she was moved by their warm welcome as Leon's new wife. Over their heads she looked at the baby. Leon caught her glance and brought Concetta over for Belle to hold. The child came to her with a sunny smile.

Belle's eyes closed tightly as she drew her close. This precious little girl was *her daughter* now! It was unbelievable.

The priest stood by with a smile, patting Concetta's head. "The *bambina* now has a beautiful new *mamma*." He made the sign of the cross over both of them.

"Thank you, Father."

They all moved out to the vestibule, where the priest asked them and the witnesses to sign the marriage document. With their signatures on it, everything was official. Leon took the baby from Belle, but as she leaned over the table to take her turn, two petals from her corsage fell on the paper. She looked around and discovered another petal still in Concetta's hand.

"She has the same sleight of hand as her *papà*. She'll need watching," Belle murmured.

His eyes gleamed molten silver. No man should be so handsome. Her hand shook as she wrote her signature. When it was done, she noticed the others were gone except for Leon. He rolled up the marriage certificate and put it in his pocket.

"Talia carried the baby out to our car. Shall we go, Signora Malatesta?"

Belle wondered if she would ever get used to her new name. He walked her outside to the church parking area.

"I looked up the meaning of your name in the library the other day, Leon. I knew *mal* meant *bad,* but found out *testa* meant *head.*" They'd reached the sedan where Talia had put the baby in the car seat. She was standing by the rear fender.

"If it meant bad people headed your family, then it had to have been a long time ago, because I've known nothing but good from your hands and your father's. I just wanted you to know that I'm proud to bear your name."

Some emotion turned his eyes a darker gray. "I'll cherish that compliment. Thank you." He helped her into the backseat next to Concetta, who was biting a plastic doughnut. Rufo lay at her feet, guarding her. Before Leon stood up, he planted a swift kiss on Belle's mouth, then shut the door. While he walked Talia to the car where the others were waiting, Belle ran a finger over her lips.

He was her husband. She needed to get used to this, but every time he touched her, she went up in flame.

In a minute he came back to the sedan. Once he was behind the wheel they drove away from the church. With the palazzo their next destination, Belle's thoughts darted to his family and their reaction when they heard the news.

Her heart ached for Leon. Though they both hoped the announcement of their marriage would help the situation with Dante, she knew her husband had been in pain over him for years. He had to be anxious right now.

"Leon?" she called to him in a burst of inspiration.

He'd been glancing at her and the baby through the rearview mirror. "Are you all right? You look worried."

"I am, because I have an idea, but I don't know how you'll feel about it."

"I won't know until you tell me."

Uh-oh. He *was* on edge. She could feel it. "The other day Mom told me Dante and his wife have their own entrance into the palazzo."

"That's right. They live in the other wing."

Her lungs constricted. "What would you think if we drove around to it first and dropped in on them, unannounced and unexpected? Under normal circumstances Dante would be the first person you'd run to with our news.

"Why don't you treat him that way instead of going through your parents? The element of surprise will catch him off guard, and might even please him if he realizes your parents don't know yet. It's worth trying— that is, if they're home."

For a long time Leon didn't say anything.

"I don't know what they do with their Saturdays," he muttered.

Belle got excited when she heard that. "Then let's find out. What's the worst he can do? Slam the door in our faces while we're standing there with Concetta? I finally faced Cliff and look what happened!"

In the mirror, Leon's eyes flashed silver fire. "I believe you've got a warrior in you. If you're willing, I think your idea is rather brilliant."

*"Grazie,"* she said in lousy Italian.

"First thing we're going to do is get you a tutor."

She laughed out loud. Miraculously, he joined her. It was the release they needed. When they entered the estate, he kept driving past the courtyard and on around to the other end. Belle saw a red sports car parked outside the entrance.

Pia's car was missing. That meant Dante was home alone. If Belle's suggestion was going to work, then it was better Pia had gone somewhere.

Leon pulled to a stop. By the time he'd gotten out, Belle had already alighted from the car with the baby in her arms. There was no hesitation on her part. Rufo rubbed against Leon's legs as they walked to the door.

When the boys were young, they had their own knock for each other. Rather than use the buzzer, Leon did what he used to do, then waited. Belle glanced at him. "Try it again."

He would have, but suddenly the door opened. To say that a disheveled Dante, clad in sweats, was shocked to see him and his entourage was probably the understatement of all time.

"Sorry to burst in on you like this, but I wanted you to be the first to know."

Dante squinted at him through eyes as dark a charcoal as their father's. "What in the hell are you talking about?"

"Belle and I just got married. We've come straight from the church."

"Be serious."

"I've never been more serious in my life."

A look of bewilderment crossed his face. "I thought you were still grieving over Benedetta."

Leon nodded. "I'll never forget her, but then something amazing happened when I met Belle. Papà is in for a shock when I tell him. You and I both know he has several women lined up, and expects me to marry one of them, but I could never do what he wants. I've never believed in titles."

A full minute passed before his brother said, "He'll tell you to annul your marriage."

"Not when he learns we fell in love the moment we met and haven't been separated since. I couldn't let her go back to New York tomorrow."

Dante took the scroll from him and unrolled it. After studying it he said, "But to marry Luciana's daughter…" His eyes darted to Belle, who was entertaining the baby.

"We've never talked about it before, but I'm convinced the same thing happened to Papà when he met Luciana."

Dante swallowed hard. "I figured that much out when I got a little older. Papà never loved Mamma that way," he muttered.

"No," Leon whispered, glad his brother had come to the same conclusion. "That's why it hurt us so damn much when he got married that fast."

"It did that, all right."

Clearing his throat, Leon said, "There's something I've been needing to say for a long time. I hurt you when I went to school in Rome. I shouldn't have left you, but I was in so much pain, I thought only of myself. I'm hoping one day you'll be able to forgive me."

Dante eyed him with soulful eyes, an expression he hadn't seen since they were teenagers, but he had no words for him. Fresh pain consumed Leon. As Belle had said, it was worth a try.

He took the certificate from him. "We're going to go tell the parents now. It would be nice if you were there for a backup. You know how Papà feels when he sees either of us let our emotions overrule what he considers our duty. If he can't handle this, then Belle and I will be moving to New York with the baby."

An odd sound came out of Dante. "You'd go that far?"

"For my wife and daughter, yes." He reached out and grasped his brother's shoulder. "Thanks for answering the door. I purposely gave it our special knock to give you the chance to open it or not. Despite what you might think, you always were and always will be my best friend."

He turned to Belle and took the baby from her. "Come on, my little *bellissima*. We'll walk around to the other end of the palazzo and enjoy this wonderful day."

# CHAPTER EIGHT

"Just a minute, Leon. I need to grab her diaper bag." When they were out of hearing range, Belle caught up to him. "No matter what happens, you spoke your piece and your brother knows you love him. It's up to him now."

Leon grasped her hand and squeezed her fingers. "That's what has me worried. Don't forget he's a Malatesta."

"Have you forgotten I'm proud to be married to one? Remember something else. He didn't slam the door in your face, either. That has to count for something."

Leon had married an angel. "Are you ready to face the parents?"

She nodded. "Be honest. You *are* a little worried about their reaction."

"You're wrong, Belle."

"Then what's the matter?"

His bride was highly perceptive, but he

couldn't tell her the truth yet. He knew the reasons she'd entered into this marriage, but she didn't know all of them. When she found out, *that* was what he was worried about.

"Your life hasn't been like anyone else's. Not even your wedding day could be like anyone else's. I—"

"There you are!" Luciana called to them, cutting off the rest of what he was going to say. "I saw your car pull around the drive, but you were so long I came to see what was going on."

Belle ran to meet her mother and they hugged. "Leon wanted to talk to Dante for a minute."

"That was an awfully long minute, when I've been waiting for you. Sullisto went to the bank this morning, but he'll be home any second." They both gravitated to the baby. "Look at that outfit she's wearing! Where have you been?"

"To church," Belle answered with her innate honesty. "We were there quite a while. She needs a diaper change and a bottle."

Leon carried Concetta into the house, deciding it was the perfect segue for what was coming. He handed her over when Belle reached for her, and all three females disappeared into one of the guest rooms, while he wandered around the living room, looking at the many family pictures.

There was an eight-by-ten that he particularly loved—his mother on her knees in the garden. She wore a broad-rimmed hat and was planting a rosebush. Flowers were her passion. So were her two boys.

She'd poured out all her love on them. In the process she'd spoiled them, but Leon could never complain. His childhood had been idyllic. That's what he wanted for Concetta. He knew Belle would love her forever.

He picked up the framed photo. "Mamma? I wish you were here today. You'd love Belle the same way you loved Benedetta."

When he heard voices, he put it back and looked across the room at the stunning picture of the three women in his life. They sat down on one of the couches while Belle fed the baby.

"I know she's so good, but I'm surprised you took her to Mass," Luciana said.

Belle flashed him a signal. He took the chair closest to the couch and pulled it around. "Not Mass. We arranged a private meeting with Father Luc."

"Why?"

"This morning your daughter did me the honor of becoming my wife." He drew the certificate out of his pocket and handed it to Luciana. "Last night we talked everything over. I asked her to marry me, so she wouldn't go back to New York and meet some other man. As you can see, Concetta is already crazy about her."

With tear-filled eyes, Luciana looked at Belle. "I only want to know one thing. Do you love him? Because if you don't, darling…"

Leon knew what Luciana was asking. She was married to a man who'd done his duty with Leon's mother, but the personal fulfillment hadn't been there. The mother in Luciana didn't want that for Belle.

"It's all right, Mom," she said with a gentle laugh. "When I first met Leon, I thought of him as the dark prince of Rimini. He frightened me, but he also thrilled me."

Her half lies thrilled *him*.

"I can understand that," Luciana murmured. "He has a lot of his father in him."

"I tried not to be attracted, but that flew out the window, because we've spent hours and hours together. Then I met Concetta. The three of us had such a wonderful time watching the dolphins we didn't want it to end, did we?" She kissed his daughter's forehead. "We saw a lot of daddies there, but none of them had your daddy's way."

"Leon has been a remarkable father." Luciana's comment made him feel more ashamed of his prior behavior toward her.

"But I guess I didn't know how deeply I felt about him until he told me he wanted to marry me," Belle went on. "The thought of turning him down and flying back to New York was too devastating to contemplate. I felt the same pain at the thought of leaving you, after having just found you."

In the next breath Luciana jumped up from the couch. First she threw her arms around Belle and the baby, then Leon. "I'm so happy with this news, I can hardly contain it."

Leon's gaze fused with his wife's. If Belle had any doubts about their marriage being the right thing to do, they were wiped away by her mother's joy.

"Your father shouldn't have left. Why isn't he home yet?"

Leon had a hunch he'd been meeting with his attorney about the adoption. While he was thinking about that, they had a visitor. To his shock, his brother entered the living room, in jeans and a sport shirt, showered and shaved. "I just got off the phone with him." *Who called whom?* "He'll be here in a minute." Dante eyed Leon. "Don't worry. I didn't spoil your surprise."

He moved over to Belle and hunkered down in front of her. The baby had fallen asleep against her shoulder. "Belated congratulations. I would have invited you in earlier, but I wasn't decent."

"If you want to know the truth, when I'm at the apartment in New York, sweats are about all I wear."

Dante grinned. "Do you run?"

"As often as I can, before work."

That was news to Leon.

"We must be soul mates. Like you, I try to get in a run, but I usually do it after work."

"Does your wife run with you?"

"Sometimes."

"We'll all have to do it together."

"I'm afraid my brother swims."

Belle nodded. "So I noticed. Like a fish, I might add. Maybe I can train him by getting him to push Concetta in her stroller at the same time."

Dante roared with laughter.

"Where is Pia, by the way?"

"Visiting her mother, but I phoned her. She'll be back soon."

"Does her family live far from here?"

"No. Only a few kilometers."

"How lucky for both of them." Belle smiled at Luciana.

"They'll never know, will they, darling."

"No."

Dante studied them. "I bet it shocked both of you when you first saw each other."

Leon hadn't seen his brother smile or act this animated in years. Belle had that effect on everyone.

"When I was at the orphanage, I used to dream about what she'd look like."

Leon got up to take the baby from her. "Little did you know you saw her every time you looked in a mirror." He kissed his little girl. "I'll go put her down in the crib." Luciana had provided one for her after she was born. Leon hadn't brought her over often enough.

"I'll go with you. We'll be right back."

"Sure you will," Dante joked.

Belle followed Leon out of the living room and down the hall to the first bedroom. He put the baby on her back and covered her with a light blanket. Belle stood next to him at the side of the crib.

He reached for her hand, too full of emotion to speak.

"So far so good," she whispered.

"A miracle has happened today. It's all because of you."

"I'm afraid it's not over yet. We still have to tell your father." She eased her hand away. "If you'll excuse me for a minute, I need to freshen up, and will meet you back in the living room."

Much as he wanted to be alone with her, this wasn't the time. With another glance at his daughter, who was sleeping peacefully, he left the bedroom, and ran into his father in the hallway. The marriage certificate was in his hand. Leon had forgotten it had been left on the coffee table.

"It seems everyone in this house knows what you've done except me," Sullisto exclaimed without preamble. "Your powers of persuasion are phenomenal, to get Belle to marry you when you don't love her. You've even convinced Luciana."

Love for his stepmother seeped into Leon.

"She's only been here three days," his father added. "What did you do? Slip something into her wine?"

Leon bristled. That was below the belt, even for the count. "No. The trick of our ancestors wouldn't work on her. She doesn't drink, smoke or indulge in drugs."

"Belle's not an ordinary woman."

"Truer words were never spoken. She's made in the image of her mother, a woman who would have married the man of her heart if he hadn't been killed…. The woman you married after Mamma died because you wanted her at all cost."

His cheeks went a ruddy color. "How dare you speak to me that way—"

"I didn't say it to be offensive, Papà. I only meant to point out that true love makes us act with our hearts, not our heads."

His father's eyes glittered with emotion, but Leon had to finish what had been started years ago. "Mamma loved another man before she obeyed her parents and married you. I have no doubts my autocratic grandfather forced you into your first marriage."

"*Basta,* Leonardo!"

"I'm almost through. I was about to say it's possible *you* loved someone before you had to do your duty. I have no way of knowing, since you never shared that with me or Dante. But given a second chance, you married for the right reason. Every man and woman born should have that privilege. Concetta will grow up being able to choose."

For once in his life, Leon's father looked utterly flummoxed.

"Would you really condemn me to a loveless marriage with one of the titled women you've picked out for me, because it's what Malatestas do?"

"You're my firstborn son."

"You were *your* father's firstborn son, too. We'll both always be the firstborn, but in the end, what does it matter? In the Middle Ages it was a system devised for the aggrandizement of wealth. Surely we've come further than that in the twenty-first century."

*"Leon is right."*

Dante had suddenly materialized, seemingly out of nowhere. Sullisto swung around. "Were you in on this, too?"

"On what?"

"This outrageous marriage of your brother's." He thrust the marriage certificate at him. "When I phoned, you said nothing."

"Because I didn't know anything. But I can tell you this. When he showed up at my door, he looked happy like I haven't seen him since before Mamma died. Let's hope Luciana didn't hear you, or she might think you don't approve of her daughter. I happen to know you do or you wouldn't have invited her to come and live with you."

"So you're in his corner now?"

"This is his wedding day, Papà."

"A wedding set up to thwart me!"

"I doubt you were on his mind when he asked Belle to marry him," Dante interjected. "Just so you know, Luciana sent me to tell you lunch is ready on the terrace."

"I couldn't eat now."

"It would hurt Luciana if you don't come. In fact, it would be the height of bad manners."

Their father scowled. "I don't recall you having any the other day."

"The other day I wasn't myself." Dante shot Leon a pleading glance. "Since then I've repented."

"Why?"

"Since I've come to realize how much I love my brother."

*Bless you, Belle, for your inspiration.*

Leon smiled at him. "That goes both ways, Dante. Why don't you two go ahead? I'll find out what's keeping Belle. Maybe the baby woke up."

Their father still looked angry as he eyed both of them before walking back down the hall toward the foyer.

Dante clapped Leon on the shoulder. "That went well," he teased, sounding like the old Dante. "See you in a minute." He rolled up the marriage certificate and handed it to him.

"I owe you." Putting it in his pocket, Leon

watched them go before he hurried into the bedroom. To his surprise, he found Belle standing at the side of the door. Rufo walked over to brush against his legs.

"I heard every word. I'm so happy you and your brother have reconciled. Between the two of you, I'm sure in time you'll be able to win your father around. Your master plan worked brilliantly, Signor Malatesta. Come on. Lunch is waiting." She slipped out the door, trailing the scent of gardenias, but she didn't look at him.

His marriage was in trouble.

He knew how deep Belle's insecurities ran. Leon had to hope his powers of persuasion were as phenomenal as his father claimed. Otherwise he was in for the kind of pain from which he sensed he'd never recover.


"Leon? How soon do you think you can arrange for TCCPI to set up a phone store here?"

Now that Concetta was awake, Belle had carried her out to the patio to play buckets with her.

He was standing by the railing, looking out at the sea. She feared he was brooding over his father. "I'll lay the groundwork next week," he told her.

"At first I couldn't believe you were serious, but since then I've found out you never joke about anything. I like a challenge. It would be interesting to see if I could make a success of it."

"What do you mean, *if?*"

Leon always complimented her. She decided it was in his nature, but she didn't deserve it. "When Mac learns I'm not coming back to the store, he'll be overjoyed, because he wants my job."

"That's probably the reason he won't get it."

She chuckled. "Spoken like a man who knows about business."

"I've been thinking about that and other things. I'll arrange to have your possessions sent from your apartment."

"Except for books and a few more clothes, I brought everything else important with me. One good thing about me. I travel light."

He didn't smile. She couldn't bring him out of his dark mood.

They'd just returned from the palazzo. Belle had forced herself to eat the fabulous meal Luciana had served them. For her mother's sake she'd acted like a new bride, and had kissed Leon several times for family pictures, while Sullisto looked on with only a comment here and there.

Pia had arrived in the midst of the festivities. Whatever Dante told her must have resonated, because she was very friendly to Belle. The party atmosphere continued after Concetta awoke from her nap and entertained everyone.

With the announcement that they were leaving to get ready for a short honeymoon, Leon brought the car around to the front. Rufo jumped inside before Belle's new husband helped her and the baby, after another hug for her mother. They left the estate and drove to the villa, where she changed into jeans and a knit top.

This was her home now, complete with the dearest, sweetest little girl on the planet and a husband to die for. There was only one thing wrong with this picture. Sullisto's words still rang in her ears.

*Your powers of persuasion are phenomenal, to get Belle to marry you when you don't love her. You've even convinced Luciana.*

*She's only been here three days. What did you do? Slip something into her wine?*

No. Leon didn't have to do any of those things. Belle had fallen instantly in love with him. He was the man she would have married no matter how long she had to wait. Of course he wasn't in love with her, but he'd been right about their desire for each other.

With every kiss over the past few days, she sensed a growing hunger from him. After having been happily married to Benedetta, it was only natural he craved the same kind of fulfillment. A man could compartmentalize his needs from his emotions.

Belle couldn't.

She loved him in all the ways possible. Today she'd made vows to be his wife. That was exactly what she would be to him. If not his love, he'd given her everything else, including a baby. There were trade-offs.

Belle could always be near her mother now. He and Dante were friends again. Sullisto was at war with himself, but it spoke volumes about how much he loved Leon, because he hadn't disowned him yet.

"Where are we going on our honeymoon?" That brought his dark head around. If she wasn't mistaken, her question had caught him off guard. "Mom offered to look after Concetta."

Leon's hand went to the back of his neck. She noticed he did that when he was weighing his thoughts carefully. "Where would you like to go?"

"Anywhere on the water. How about you? Or did you do that with Benedetta…?"

"No. We honeymooned in Switzerland, but I don't want to talk about her."

"I'm sorry. Would you rather we postponed a trip right now? Believe me, I'd understand."

"Understand what?" he blurted. "My father hurt you today. Do you think I'm going to forget that?"

"I didn't take it personally, not after his warm welcome the first night we met. He needs time. You're trying to change someone who was raised under a different set of rules."

Leon's eyes narrowed on her face. "How do you know so much about people?"

"Probably because I wasn't one of the participants of life. As I've told you before, most of the time I spent it observing other people. You learn a lot that way." She cocked her head. "Does your family own a yacht?"

"Yes. Shall we take it across the water to Croatia? There are some wonderful ruins in Dubrovnik and Split to explore."

"That sounds thrilling, but this is your honeymoon, too. Since you've probably done everything, what would be your very favorite thing to do?"

His lips twitched for the first time. "That's a loaded question to ask a new husband."

"Humor me. I'm a new wife."

"Has anyone ever told you *you* live dangerously?"

Belle laughed. "I'm still waiting for your answer."

"Find a deserted island in the cruiser and do whatever appeals."

Her heart ran away with her. "An island? I'm glad you said that. I'll phone Mom and ask her to come over while we're gone. Concetta will be happier in her own surroundings, with the dog and familiar staff."

Belle picked up the baby, who'd become bored with the buckets. "Can we leave soon? It will give us more daylight to find the right island." That suggestion seemed to galvanize him into action. "I can see by your eyes you already have one in mind."

He actually grinned. When he did that, she was reduced to mush. "There's not much I can hide from you."

Yes, he could. He did! But being a Malatesta gave him special powers that rendered him inscrutable at times. Such as when he was pretending to be in love with her.

"I'll call Mom."

"While you do that, I'll pack the cruiser."

They pulled away from the dock at four, loaded with everything Leon could think of to make this trip one they'd never forget. Belle had been humoring him, to the point he could almost believe her gratitude to him for uniting her with Luciana wasn't all she was feeling.

He hoped like hell her physical response to him so far wasn't a total act. If a woman as genuine as Belle could be playing a part for his benefit, then he no longer trusted his own judgment.

They headed farther down the coast. There were no islands of volcanic origin close to Rimini, but there was a sandbar. Those familiar with the area knew to avoid it. Others came upon it too quickly and in many cases ruined their hulls. Years ago Leon had come across it by accident and got in some of the best fishing of his life. If he'd had Belle with him back then…

Using his binoculars, Leon found the exact spot. He cut the motor and let momentum carry them all the way in. When sand stopped the cruiser, Belle gazed at him in surprise. "I thought we were going to an island."

"I lied. There isn't one around here. But with the sea this calm, there's enough sand exposed for us to sunbathe until tonight, and then moon bathe under the stars. No one else is around here for miles." He loved how she'd piled her hair up on her head. "If we'd taken the yacht, we'd have staff to contend with. These days it's almost impossible to get away from people."

Her mouth curved into a smile. "But you managed it." She stood up on the bench and looked around. "I love it! It's like being shipwrecked."

"Except that we have all the comforts of home on board and can leave when we feel like it."

"I don't want to talk about leaving. We just got here. I think this is the most romantic place for a honeymoon I ever heard of. Unique in all the world." The light in her eyes dazzled him. He wanted this to be real. "A little focaccia, a bottle of water and thou. It's evident Omar Khayyám hadn't been to the Adriatic."

Laughter rumbled deep in Leon's chest before he picked her up and lifted her out of the boat to the sand. She started stripping as she ran. He did, too. They'd both worn their swimming suits beneath their clothes.

"If you'll stay close to me in the water, I won't make you wear a life preserver."

She sobered. "That rule applies to you, too, Leon. If you decide to go out alone, I don't want anything to happen to you."

*Belle...*

"Come on," he said in a husky voice when he could find it. They waded into the water, then started swimming. He loved her little shouts of excitement every time she saw a fish.

Several times they went in and out of the water, lying in the sun in between dips. Belle put on sunscreen and gathered some seashells. Leon got out his fishing pole and caught two mackerel. They cooked them in a pan on his camp stove, and ate them with salad and fruit brought from the villa. She declared she'd never eaten a tastier meal, and he agreed with her.

After the sun went down they covered up and lay back on lounge chairs on the cruiser. He turned his head so he could look at her. "When you told me earlier I'd probably done everything, you were wrong. I've never been here with anyone else."

"I'm glad you're making a new memory.

I'm really glad it's with me. This has turned out to be the most fabulous wedding day a girl could ever want. To be surrounded by your family and my own mother. I can hardly express it." Belle's voice had caught in her throat.

"You're easy company, Belle. I've never enjoyed anyone more."

"I feel the same way about you." She sat up abruptly. "Do you know I almost didn't go to your bank? Obviously the manager at Donatello Diamonds had advised me to go there for a reason, but I was so upset with him, I had to have a long talk with myself first."

Leon didn't even want to think about it, and turned on his side toward her. "What decided you in the end?"

"I knew that if I went home not being able to find my mother, it would haunt me that I hadn't turned over that one stone to see what was under it." Her way of expressing herself enchanted him.

"Tomorrow it will be a week since I flew out of JFK Airport, a single woman with no family, on a quest so overwhelming, I can't believe I followed through. Tonight I'm lying under the stars on the Adriatic with my Italian husband, knowing my mother is home watching your little girl."

"*Our* little girl now."

Belle nodded. "I know I'm not dreaming, but you have to admit the chances of all this happening are astronomical. You've been so good to me, Leon. If I spend my whole life thanking you, it won't be enough. I promise to be the best wife I can. Do you mind if I go downstairs now and take a shower? I'm a sandy mess."

"While you do that, I'll get everything battened down for the night."

Belle gathered up her things and went down the stairs to the lower deck. The twenty-one-foot cruiser had to be state-of-the-art. Leon had told her he liked a smaller boat like this. He could man it himself, and pull in and out of coves with ease. It made a lot of sense.

Beyond the galley was a cabin with a double bed. One glance at it and her heartbeat tripled. She hurriedly took a shower and washed her hair.

Leon was giving her plenty of time, but now that she was ready, she felt feverish, waiting for him to come. Belle was the only one of her roommates or the girls at her work who hadn't been to bed with a man. Now it was her turn.

The mechanics of the act were no mystery

to her, but it was a whole new world she was about to enter. Those few kisses they'd exchanged had already thrilled her, so much she couldn't wait to find out what it would be like to spend the night with him.

They hadn't talked about the consequences of sleeping together, but she'd made a vow to accept children lovingly. How would he feel about another child if she conceived? Or was Concetta enough for him?

This marriage had happened so fast, Belle was full of questions about the sexual side of their relationship. Only he could answer them. Why didn't he come? They needed to talk.

After another five minutes, she walked down through the hallway and called to him from the stairs.

"I'll be right there."

When he joined her in the bedroom five minutes later, he'd showered and was dressed in a T-shirt and lounging pajamas. The sight of his black hair disheveled after being washed had an appeal all its own. Her gaze dropped lower, to that well-defined physique she'd longed to touch all day. He was standing only a few feet away. She could reach out and touch him. Marriage had given her the right, but she needed a signal from him.

"Is there anything you need before I go back up on deck for the night?"

The question, asked in that deep voice, sent her down a dark chute with no bottom. The pain was so acute she couldn't hold it in. "I thought this was to be our wedding night."

His sudden grim expression chilled her, reminding her of the side of his nature that could be forbidding at times. "Under normal circumstances it would be."

She shook her head, causing her hair to swish across her shoulders. "These aren't normal? I don't understand."

For a moment she thought she saw a bleak look enter his eyes, but it might have been a trick of light. "You don't have to keep up the pretense any longer, Belle."

"Excuse me?"

"Your gratitude has been duly recognized. The truth is, I don't expect your sleeping with me to be a part of it."

She sucked in her breath. "Well, pardon me if I misunderstood. I thought this morning we took vows to become man and wife. You know—the kind who sleep together."

Now that she was all worked up, she couldn't stop. "You think you're so different from your father, but you're just another version of the same male. He was right. You don't love me. *That* I can handle. You've taught me that love at first sight is an absurdity, after all. I learn something new every day.

"Everyone knows real love takes years and years to develop. It's your lie about feeling desire for me that cuts to the quick, Leonardo di Malatesta. You faked it until I believed it, but now that it's crunch time, you've brushed me off the way I've been brushed off all my life."

*"Belle—"* A ring of white had encircled his hard mouth.

"I'm not finished. Do you have any idea how hurt I am by your rejection? How humiliated I feel after putting everything I am and feel out there on the line for you?

"Cliff was right about my being pathetic. Thank you for underscoring what I've always known about myself. But until just now I was looking forward to being with you tonight, to being in your arms.

"I thought my stepfather hurt me when he told me to get out of his garage and never step in it again. But you're the true master at turning the knife. Now that you've drawn blood, please leave *my* bedroom. We'll never talk about this again.

"In the morning I want to go back to the

villa. Never fear, I'll go on being your wife and a mother to Concetta. I'll be there for your family day and night. You want to sleep in the same bed to keep up the pretense and avoid gossip? I'll do it. I'll stand by you at work, at home, until death. I owe you that. I made vows to do that."

She took a deep, painful breath. "But don't you *ever* touch me in bed, not even by accident."

Leon hadn't been sick to his stomach in years. But at two in the morning he slipped over the side of the boat and found a private spot. After being violently ill, he shook like a man with palsy. Until she heard him out, he wasn't going to make it through the night.

He decided it would be better to make noise on his way below deck so he wouldn't frighten her. Once he reached the bathroom, he brushed his teeth and drank some water. Then he tapped on the closed door. "Belle?"

"What is it?"

"We can't go on like this. I have to talk to you. May I come in, or do we do this through the door?"

"It's your boat."

It didn't sound as if she'd been asleep. He opened the door and a dim beam of light from the hallway fell across the bed, where her dark hair was splayed across the pillow. She was an enticing vision. How to begin repairing the damage?

Leon reached the end of the bed and sat on it. "When I came down here earlier, the last thing I wanted to do was go back upstairs for the night. But because of the speed of our marriage, I didn't want you to think that I'd 'purchased' you so I could claim my rights. I wanted to give you time to get used to me.

"Today was pure enchantment for me. I wanted it to go on and on. I was terrified that if you knew how much I'd been counting the minutes until we could go to bed together, it would frighten you. So I backed off. But to my despair, I unwittingly made the wrong decision, and I fear it has cost me my marriage.

"You have no idea how sick I was when I realized you'd overheard the conversation with my father. When we went into lunch, I knew the things he'd said had affected you. I felt helpless to do anything about it until I could get you alone. But when I came down the stairs to join you after your shower, I saw a woman who looked like the proverbial lamb going to slaughter.

"I thought of your bravery in leaving

the orphanage to go to a strange home and adapt to someone else's lifestyle. You were so strong to do that and be able to handle it. Tonight I saw your strength in the way you faced me head-on, no matter what you might be feeling inside.

"Your trust in me was so humbling, I didn't want to do anything wrong. You have to understand I would never deliberately hurt you. How could I do that?" He tipped his head back. "There's something important you need to know, Belle."

"What is it?"

"This is about my mother. She had some last words for me before she died. I'll never forget them."

Belle stirred in the bed. "What did she tell you?"

"She said, 'You're so much like me, Leon. If you expect to ever truly be happy, then follow your heart.' Her advice sank deep inside me and helped free me from certain expectations, because I knew I had her blessing. When the time came to ask Benedetta to marry me, I didn't hesitate.

"Last night I asked you to marry me for the same reason. The *only* reason. I love you, Belle. I'm a man desperately in love. You're the most beautiful thing in my life. When we said our vows this morning, I kept thanking God for you in my heart. I can't explain why I fell so hard for you. The French have an expression for it—*coup de foudre.* A bolt of lightning. That's what it was like for me.

"Immediately I needed an excuse to keep you here for good. But the truth is, if there'd been no excuse—no baby, no Dante, no mother to find—I would have followed you back to New York until I could get you to fall in love with me."

Leon moved to the door, petrified he wasn't making any headway. "As God is my witness, I love you. That's what I came to say."

He walked into the hallway and was about to shut the door when he heard the rustle of sheets. "Don't leave me."

Afraid he was hearing things, he turned around in time to see Belle move toward him. "Don't ever leave me." In seconds he felt her arms around his neck. "I'm madly in love with you, too, Leon. I love you so much it hurts. Don't you know that's why I said those cruel things to you?"

He came close to expiring with joy. "I do now." He picked her up in his arms and carried her back to bed, following her down with his body. The second their mouths fused, they began devouring each other.

Belle awakened the next morning before her husband. She lay halfway across his chest, with their legs entangled, and watched him in sleep. He was the most beautiful man she'd ever seen.

She loved his powerful legs, which kept her where he wanted her, even in sleep. The top cover lay on the floor, along with her robe and his clothes. She hadn't known pleasure like they'd given each other was even possible. It was too intoxicating to describe.

Unable to hold back, she kissed his eyelids and nose, the cleft in his chin. It was embarrassing how much she wanted him again. "Darling," she said against his compelling mouth, "are you awake?"

His hand roved over her back.

Delighted with that much response, she kissed his throat and worked her way to one earlobe. She slid her fingers into his black hair. Belle was on fire for him. "I love you," she cried, out of need for the fulfillment only he could give. Her dark prince had to be the most satisfying lover alive.

His eyes opened at last. They were smoldering like wood smoke. *"Buon giorno, esposa mia."*

She smiled. "It will be a very good morning when you've made love to me again."

He rolled her on top of him so he could look up at her. "You're a shameless beauty. How lucky can a husband be?"

"Was last night as wonderful for you as it was for me?"

Belle heard him take a ragged breath. "Couldn't you tell? I ate you alive last night."

She smiled. "I'm still alive," she said breathlessly.

"I know. Come here to me, *bellissima.*"

It was several hours later when they surfaced. Leon kept a possessive arm around her hips while they stared into each other's eyes. "Where do you want to go today?"

"I want to stay right here. Is that all right with you?"

He laughed out loud. "You don't know much about men, but I have to admit I'm thankful I'm your first and only lover."

She traced the line of his mouth with her finger. It could go soft or hard depending on his mood. Right now there was a sensual curl. "I could look at you for hours. Do you think I'm terrible?"

He laughed again. "As long as I get to do the same thing."

Heat rose to her cheeks. "I think it's fun to be married. After being with you like this, I realize I grew up lonely. It worries me that I might be too needy. Promise you'll help me not to get that way."

He smoothed the hair away from her temple. "I think you're perfect just as you are."

"That's because we're on our honeymoon. But when you have to go to the bank, I don't think I'll be able to let you leave. Concetta and I will be miserable until you get home. Will you hate it if I bring lunch to your office sometimes?"

"What do you think?"

"I think you will."

After another burst of laughter he kissed her passionately.

"Leon?" she said, when he finally let her catch her breath. "I've given the idea of the cell phone store a lot of thought. The truth is I'd really like to be a full-time mother to Concetta. In order to do that, I couldn't manage a store, too."

He kissed a certain spot. "Especially if we decided we wanted to have another baby."

"You'd like that?"

"I want one with you. Concetta needs

a sibling. My life was rich because I had Dante."

"You were lucky to have a brother. When do you think you'd like to try for a baby?"

Leon's shoulders shook with silent laughter. "Whenever you think you can handle it."

"If we tried pretty soon and were successful, that would make the babies maybe a year and a half apart. That would be perfect."

"Whatever you say, *squisita*."

"You're laughing at me."

Leon grew serious. "No. I'm laughing because I'm so happy. The dark period I went through with Benedetta's illness and death took its toll. At the time I couldn't imagine feeling like I do right now. You've brought sunshine back into my life."

"You don't have time to hear all the things you've done for me—not before I feed you. While you lie here and miss me like crazy, I'm going to fix you breakfast in bed."

She tried to get up, but he pulled her back. "Don't leave me, Belle."

She pressed a hungry kiss to his mouth. "I'll only be as far away as the galley."

"That's too far."

"Now you know why I'm already dreading you going to work. I've decided I think it's scary to be married."

He took her face between his hands. "I've decided I adore you, Signora Malatesta."

# CHAPTER NINE

*Three months later*

USING THE FRONT door key she'd been given, Belle let herself and Concetta inside the palazzo. She'd put her adorable baby in the stroller. "Mom? We're here!"

No answer. That was odd. After Sullisto had left for the bank, her mother had called asking her to come over. Luciana wanted help putting the finishing touches on the birthday party she was planning for Leon's father that evening.

"Mom? Where are you?" She walked through the house, pushing Concetta. "Hmm, maybe she's out in the garden picking flowers. Let's go find your grandmother."

Belle was dying to talk to her mom and was thankful for the excuse to come over now. Leon had arranged for an early business meeting so he could get home in good time for the party, so she was free.

The housekeeper saw her in the hallway. "*Buon giorno,* Belle. Your *mamma* is still in the bed."

Uh-oh. That didn't sound like her mother. "*Grazie,* Violeta."

Belle pushed the stroller through the house to the master suite. She opened the door. "Mom?"

"Come in the bedroom, darling."

Curious, Belle hurried on through and found a slightly pale version of her beautiful mother lying against the pillows. "You're sick, aren't you."

"Not the kind I can give to Concetta. It's a good kind."

A *good* kind of sick?

*What?* All of a sudden Belle got it. She gazed down at her mother. "You're *pregnant!*"

"*Yes...*"

Belle sank down on the side of the bed. "Does Sullisto know?"

"No. He thinks I've got a bug of some kind."

"You *do!*" They both started laughing and then Belle hugged her mother in happiness. They stared hard at each other. "After all this time…" Belle looked at the baby. "Did you hear that, Concetta? In about seven months you're going to get a new aunt or uncle."

The two of them laughed for joy again before Luciana's eyes filled with tears. "It took finding you, darling. That's what the doctor said. You don't know how much I've wanted us to have a baby together, even if I am forty-two. You know, to cement things. This morning Sullisto almost didn't leave for work. I had to beg him to go."

Belle could relate, which was a change for her where Leon was concerned. But this wasn't the time to confide in Luciana. "How long have you had morning sickness?"

"For a few days. I've sworn Violeta to secrecy."

"Until tonight?"

"Yes. The doctor gave me some antinausea medicine. It's already starting to work."

"Sullisto's going to jump out of his skin with joy."

"I believe he will."

"I *know* he will. He loves you terribly, Mom, but being a Malatesta he wants everything to be perfect."

Her father-in-law had calmed down somewhat since Belle and Leon had come back from their honeymoon on the sandbar. But whether he'd forgiven his son for disobeying him a second time was something no one knew.

"Ah, you've already discovered that after being married to Leon. So tell me what's on your mind, darling, and don't say it's nothing."

Belle bit her lip. "When Concetta and I came over this morning, there was something I wanted to talk to you about, but now I can't."

"You mean that you're pregnant, too?"

Her breath caught. "Oh, Mom… I think I am, but I haven't done a home pregnancy test yet. That's what I wanted to discuss with you."

"I've suspected it since our family picnic the other day, when you couldn't eat."

"I didn't realize you'd noticed. If I thought I was carrying Leon's child…"

"Then he doesn't suspect yet?"

"No. I've had a few bouts of nausea, nothing terrible yet, but lately I'm so tired."

Her mother's delightful laugh filled the room. "You need to test yourself right now. There's a kit in my closet, hidden behind the shoes."

"You're kidding!"

"No. I bought two just in case. But the first one worked."

"I'll be right back."

"While you get the official word, I'm going to entertain my granddaughter. Come here, Concetta, and give your pregnant grandmother a big kiss."

Belle found the kit and went into the bathroom. A few minutes later she squealed for joy. Though she was barely learning the rudiments of Italian from her husband and the staff, she didn't need to read the words to understand what the color meant. She ran into the bedroom to show her mother.

"Congratulations, darling! Now that everything's official, we'll make our announcements tonight."

"We can't do that in front of Pia, Mom. It will hurt her too much."

"No, it won't. I know something you don't."

Belle blinked in shock and took the baby from her. "Are you teasing me?"

"No. She told me yesterday."

*Yesterday...* Belle was so excited, she could hardly stand it. "Does she know about you?"

"Yes, but our husbands don't know yet. Obviously, yours doesn't, either." Her mother flashed a secretive smile. "We decided to make this a real surprise party tonight. To know you're pregnant, too… Three in one family at the same time has to be some kind of world record."

"I agree. How do you want to handle it?"

"I think it should be something that shocks our husbands. You know how they love to be in control at all times. It's a Malatesta trait. Don't you think it would be fun just this once to throw them off base?"

She had an imp in her that Belle would never have guessed was there. "There's nothing I'd love more." She'd been standing by a window that overlooked the maze. Suddenly her brain started reeling with possibilities. "In fact, I've got an idea. First we're going to need poster board and hundreds of yards of ribbon in three colors."

"What on earth do you have in mind, darling?"

"A game. We love games, don't we, Concetta." She kissed her daughter's cheeks. "This one is going to be for all the men in the family to play. But this game will be different, because each man will end up getting the prize he's always wanted."

After a successful business meeting, Leon rushed home early to be with his family. The party wasn't scheduled to start for an hour and a half. That would give him enough time to enjoy his wife while his daughter had her nap. Up until this morning, when Belle had stayed asleep, she'd always been so loving and responsive, he knew he was the luckiest man on earth.

Disappointment washed over him in waves when he walked in and Simona informed him that everyone had left for the palazzo hours ago. The news hit him like a body blow. He'd been longing to lie in Belle's arms and forget the world for a little while. She made him feel immortal.

As he took the stairs two at a time to the master bedroom, he realized how empty the villa was without them. The thought of no Belle, his creative, adorable wife, was anathema to him.

All Leon had to do was shower and shave. He and Dante had gone in on a gift for their father. Sullisto had mislaid his old watch and hadn't found it yet, so they'd bought him a new one with their names engraved in it. Dante would be bringing it to the party.

For the occasion Leon had bought himself a new, light gray suit. Belle had told him several times how much she liked him in gray, the color of his eyes. Hating the silence of the house, he hurriedly dressed, and drove to the palazzo at a speed over the limit. He never drove this fast with Belle and Concetta, but he was in a hurry to see them.

When he pulled up in front, he saw his father and brother waiting for him in the courtyard, dressed in what looked like new suits. Leon levered himself from the driver's seat.

"*Buon compleanno,* Papà." He kissed him on both cheeks. "What's going on? Why are you out here?"

"We've been given our instructions, Leonardo." Sullisto didn't sound in the least happy.

Dante's dark brows lifted. "We were told to stay out here, and that when you got here, we were to go to the entrance of the maze to await further instructions."

Leon chuckled. He thought he could see his playful wife's hand in this somewhere. "Where's my family?"

"They're all inside," his father muttered, looking flustered. "Let's get this foolishness over with."

"It *is* your birthday, Papà."

"You're just going to have to be a good sport even if you are a year older," Dante teased.

They headed through the vine-covered

gate to the maze. "I told Luciana I didn't want any fuss," Sullisto grumbled.

When they reached the entrance, there was a sign in Italian. Start Following Your Ribbon. Red for Sullisto, Yellow for Dante and Blue for Leon. Don't Open Your Prizes When You Find Them. Bring Them to the Terrace, Where More Festivities Will Ensue.

Hmm. A prize. Just what did Leon's wife have in store for him? For the first time in years he got the kind of excited feeling he used to get as a child when his mother hid something they wanted, and they had to find it. He put a hand on his father's shoulder. "You go first, Papà."

"For the love of heaven," Sullisto mumbled.

With a grin, Dante followed him.

Leon brought up the rear. The ribbons led them on such a serpentine route, he started laughing. Dante joined in. Their father had gone on ahead and had disappeared. He just wanted to get the game over with.

"This is one game we never played in here," his brother quipped.

"Nope." And Leon knew why. Belle hadn't grown up with them. Her advent in his life had changed his entire world. "I guess this is where we part company. My ribbon has taken off in a new direction. See you in a minute."

"Call out if you get lost."

"That'll be the day, little brother."

Leon kept going until he came to a small package on the ground tied up with the end of the ribbon. Picking it up, he followed the ribbon back to the opening of the maze. Pretty soon his father emerged with an identical package.

"I think Dante must have gotten lost."

"I heard that, big brother." In the next breath Dante made his appearance with his own package.

Sullisto muttered, "I hope this is the end of the games. I don't know about you, but I'm hungry."

The three of them walked around to the terrace with the ribbons trailing behind.

"Careful you don't trip on those," Luciana called out from the table, looking particularly radiant in an ice-blue dress. "Happy birthday, my darling husband."

Pia sat next to her in a stunning pink outfit.

Leon's gaze sought his wife, who was wearing a gorgeous purple dress with spaghetti straps. She was so beautiful he almost dropped his package.

Luciana smiled at all of them. "As soon as you open your gifts, we'll eat."

Her smile was like the cat who'd swallowed the proverbial canary. Something was going on....

Leon opened his package. Inside was a small oblong box containing a home pregnancy device, of all things. His heart thundered in his chest before he even looked inside it. Belle's cobalt eyes had found his. They resembled blue fires, telling him everything that was in her heart.

It came to him then that everyone on the terrace had gone silent. When he looked around, he saw that both his brother and his father held similar boxes in their hands, and were totally dumbstruck.

Sullisto raised his head and looked at Luciana. "We're pregnant?" he whispered in awe.

"Yes, darling. It finally happened."

The look on his father's face was one Leon would never forget.

Pia's beaming countenance told its own story as she eyed Dante with loving eyes. "That trip to Florence," she reminded him.

Suddenly pandemonium struck.

Leon dropped the box and gravitated

to his wife, pulling her from the seat into his arms.

"Concetta won't be an only child," she said against his lips. "I hope you're happy, Leon."

"Happy?" he cried. *"Ti amo, amore mio. Ti amo!"* He kissed her long and hard.

It was in this euphoric condition that he heard his father tap the crystal goblet in front of him with a fork to get their attention. Everyone broke apart and sat down while Sullisto remained standing. He lifted his wineglass toward Belle.

He had to clear his throat several times. "To my wife's firstborn, who came like an angel from across the ocean to bless the Houses of Malatesta and Donatello forever and make us all one."

"Hear, hear," an ecstatic Dante echoed, raising his glass.

Leon gripped Belle's thigh beneath the table with one hand, and picked up his wineglass with the other. "Amen and amen."

\* \* \* \* \*

### Available September 3, 2013

## #4391 BOUND BY A BABY
### by Kate Hardy
Becoming guardian to her orphaned godson is a heartbreaking honor for Emmy Jacobs. The real challenge will be sharing that honor with brooding godfather Dylan Harper!

## #4392 IN THE LINE OF DUTY
### by Ami Weaver
Ex-soldier Matt Bowden is used to burying his feelings for Callie Marshall, but now everything has changed. Is he the risk she's been holding out for?

## #4393 PATCHWORK FAMILY IN THE OUTBACK
*Bellaroo Creek* • by Soraya Lane
When teacher Poppy Carter arrives in Bellaroo Creek, she knows it will be a hard task. But single father Harrison Black proves the biggest test of all!

## #4394 STRANDED WITH THE TYCOON
### by Sophie Pembroke
Ben Hampton is the last man Luce would *ever* choose to be stranded with. But after getting snowbound in the countryside, will their attraction prove irresistible?

---

HRLPCNM0813

# LARGER-PRINT BOOKS!

## GET 2 FREE LARGER-PRINT NOVELS PLUS
# 2 FREE GIFTS!

### ⊞ HARLEQUIN®

*Romance*

### From the Heart, For the Heart

**YES!** Please send me 2 FREE LARGER-PRINT Harlequin® Romance novels and my 2 FREE gifts (gifts are worth about $10). After receiving them, if I don't wish to receive any more books, I can return the shipping statement marked "cancel." If I don't cancel, I will receive 4 brand-new novels every month and be billed just $4.84 per book in the U.S. or $5.24 per book in Canada. That's a savings of at least 19% off the cover price! It's quite a bargain! Shipping and handling is just 50¢ per book in the U.S. and 75¢ per book in Canada.* I understand that accepting the 2 free books and gifts places me under no obligation to buy anything. I can always return a shipment and cancel at any time. Even if I never buy another book, the two free books and gifts are mine to keep forever.

119/319 HDN F43Y

Name _____ (PLEASE PRINT)

Address _____ Apt. #

City _____ State/Prov. _____ Zip/Postal Code

Signature (if under 18, a parent or guardian must sign)

### Mail to the **Harlequin® Reader Service:**
**IN U.S.A.:** P.O. Box 1867, Buffalo, NY 14240-1867
**IN CANADA:** P.O. Box 609, Fort Erie, Ontario L2A 5X3
**Want to try two free books from another line?**
**Call 1-800-873-8635 or visit www.ReaderService.com.**

* Terms and prices subject to change without notice. Prices do not include applicable taxes. Sales tax applicable in N.Y. Canadian residents will be charged applicable taxes. Offer not valid in Quebec. This offer is limited to one order per household. Not valid for current subscribers to Harlequin Romance Larger-Print books. All orders subject to credit approval. Credit or debit balances in a customer's account(s) may be offset by any other outstanding balance owed by or to the customer. Please allow 4 to 6 weeks for delivery. Offer available while quantities last.

**Your Privacy**—The Harlequin® Reader Service is committed to protecting your privacy. Our Privacy Policy is available online at www.ReaderService.com or upon request from the Harlequin Reader Service.

We make a portion of our mailing list available to reputable third parties that offer products we believe may interest you. If you prefer that we not exchange your name with third parties, or if you wish to clarify or modify your communication preferences, please visit us at www.ReaderService.com/consumerchoice or write to us at Harlequin Reader Service Preference Service, P.O. Box 9062, Buffalo, NY 14269. Include your complete name and address.

HRLP13R

"Can we get this, as well? I think Tyler'd love it."

"You mean, *you* love it." Emmy seemed to like simple, childlike things. And Dylan hadn't quite worked out yet whether he found that more endearing or annoying. He certainly didn't loathe her as much as he once had. She was good with the baby, too.

Her eyes crinkled at the corners. "Okay, then, let's ask him." She picked up the cot toy, crouched down beside the pram, switched it on and let Tyler see the lights and hear the lullaby.

Tyler's eyes went wide. Then he laughed and held his hands out toward it.

Emmy looked up at him and smiled. "I think that's a yes."

Again a surge of attraction hit him. Was he crazy? This was Emmy Jacobs, who sparred with him and sniped at him and was his co-guardian. She was the last person he wanted to get involved with. But at the same time he had to acknowledge that there was something about her that really got under his skin. Something that made him want to know more about her. Get closer.

And that in itself was weird. He didn't do close. Never had.

He didn't trust anyone to let them near enough.

The rest of the weekend turned out to be Dylan's first weekend of being a dad. Although it was officially Emmy's weekend on duty, he somehow ended up going to the park with her to take Tyler out for some fresh air. He noticed that she talked to Tyler all the time, even though there was no way a baby could possibly understand everything she said. She pointed out flowers and named the colors for him; she pointed out dogs and birds and squirrels.

She was clearly taking her duties as godmother and guardian really seriously, and Dylan was beginning to wonder just why he'd ever disliked her so much. Then again, this new Emmy didn't have a smart-aleck mouth. She didn't snipe, and she wasn't cynical and hard-bitten like the Emmy Jacobs he was used to.

Which one was the real Emmy? he wondered. Was she letting her guard down and letting him see the real her? Or was this just some kind of mirage and Spiky Emmy would return to drive him crazy?

*BOUND BY A BABY by Kate Hardy*
*is available September 2013 only from*
*Harlequin Romance—don't miss it!*